Homecoming

By

Orlando A. Sanchez

A Montague & Strong Detective Novel

Home is that sigh for a color of sky and a will to return. Robert A. Heinlein

This one is for my Dad.

I lost you a long time ago and my memories, vague as they are always place you as larger than life in my mind's eye. I wish you could have been here to see us all grow up, to handle all of your grandkids and see your legacy.

I still remember your smile, your laugh, and your enormous hands when you would lift me up to stand on your shoulders. Every time you placed me there I felt like a giant.

I like to think I'm still standing there now, making you proud.

Copyright © 2018 by Orlando A. Sanchez

Published by Bitten Peaches Publishing NY NY

Cover Design by Deranged Doctor Design
www.derangeddoctordesign.com

ONE

"IGNISCORUSCANTI," I WHISPERED, forming an orb of violet energy. It was about the size of a grapefruit and it hovered in my palm. I felt the energy race up my arm and suffuse my body with warmth. I held it in front of me, and Peaches shifted mid-sprawl to look up at me.

<Are you going to make magic meat?>

"This is an incantation orb," I answered, keeping my focus on the sphere of magical energy in my hand.

Peaches turned away, disinterested, and chuffed. I focused on the orb, trying to channel more energy into it. I saw it start to expand, but then it rapidly collapsed to the size of a grape.

"Shit."

It floated out of my palm and onto the floor. Peaches turned again, lifted one massive paw, crushed it and snapped it up in one gulp.

<That's not very good. Can you make the magic meat?>

I felt a surge of energy and a rift opened behind us. I looked back as Monty stepped through.

"That's a new look for you." I noticed the missing jacket and rips along the sleeves of his shirt. His pants didn't look much better, being torn in several places as well. "What's this called—'mangled mage'?"

"*This* used to be a Zegna Bespoke." Monty pointed to his clothes with an irritated look. "I need a cuppa."

"How'd it go?"

"Tea." He held up a hand, walked into the kitchen, and put the kettle on. "Redrum was being modified and the homeless were being forced to take it against their will."

"Shit, that sounds bad," I said, joining him in the kitchen. "Do we need to mobilize?"

"No need," he answered. "It's mostly contained. I think Stryder will pursue this to its resolution."

"How was the Redrum modified?"

Monty took the whistling kettle off the stove and poured the water into a cup. "Someone managed to introduce an ultraviolet resistance into the composition of the blood, altering it to allow rummers to traverse during the day."

"UV-resistant rummers?"

"Precisely." He took a sip of his Earl Grey. "It gets worse, Simon."

"What could possibly be worse than rummers out during the day?"

"Hades gave *Kokutan no ken* to Grey Stryder."

"What? What the hell is a Grey Stryder, some kind of sneaker?" I asked.

Monty gave me the 'are you truly this clueless' look. "Grey Stryder is a Night Warden."

"So let's ask Mr. Grey Sneaker for the sword before

the Dark Council decides to shred each other."

"Stryder has bonded to the sword by now, if he isn't dead."

"Why does that sound much worse than sparkly rummers?" I asked. "Is this Stryder going to be a problem?"

"He's one of the last—if not *the* last—Night Wardens," Monty replied. "He's difficult but governed by a sense of justice and a rigid moral code."

"Aren't the Night Wardens mages?" I asked. "How did he manage the bond without being erased?"

Monty put the cup down and rubbed his chin in thought.

"An entropic dissolution," he answered, as if I knew what he meant. "Made him the perfect vessel. Who knew?"

"Not me. Did you ask his godness, Hades, why he gave away the sword that can keep the Dark Council from tearing itself apart?"

Monty shook his head. "Hades is playing a long-game here, but I don't know what it is, and I can't see why he would make this move. Code or no code, Stryder is a serious threat."

"Do we postpone the homecoming?"

Monty looked up at me. "No. I need to get back to the Sanctuary before Oliver sends more Ghosts to convince me that death is a good idea."

"And this Oliver is a fan because…?"

"I don't know." He looked down at his ruined clothes. "I need to change. Have you heard from my uncle?"

"Not since London. Are you opening a rift to the

Sanctuary, or do we need to do the digestive destruction of a teleportation circle?"

"Neither. The Sanctuary has defensive measures in place to prevent direct teleportation," Monty said. "There is a hundred-square-mile magical dead zone around it."

"What are we going to do?" I asked. "Walk up to the front door and knock? 'Hello? We're here to storm the castle!'"

"There's an airport ten miles from the Sanctuary portal." Monty headed to the back rooms. "We're flying there."

"Flying? As in a plane?"

"Have you achieved the power of autonomous flight?"

"Not lately, even though it felt like that in London."

"Then we're flying—in a plane."

A crashing sound came from Dex's room, followed by a bright green flash that spilled out from beneath the door. Peaches immediately stood and padded over, waiting. Dex stepped out and stumbled a few steps into the office.

"Ach, that Morrigan is one fiery woman!" he shouted. "Barely escaped with my loins intact."

He gave me a wide grin and slapped me on the back.

"Glad to hear you and the Morrigan are doing so well, I think?"

"Good to see you, boy. Where's my ever-pleasant nephew?"

Dex gestured and materialized two large sausages for Peaches, who proceeded to happily inhale them.

<Ask him to teach you how to make the magic meat. This

tastes better than your glowing ball.>

"At least say thank you," I muttered under my breath and shook my head. "You massive black hole."

Peaches stepped close to Dex and nudged him with his head, slamming him into the wall. Dex bounced off the wall, rubbing his abdomen.

"Ach, that's a good hellhound." He patted Peaches' head with a chuckle. "Now, where's Tristan?"

"Getting dressed." I pointed to the back room. "He had a run-in with some rummers."

"Nasty business, that," Dex said, pushing my head down as a huge raven soared into the room. "Careful, you daft bird! Apologies."

Herk, Dex's raven companion, perched on top of one of the chairs in the reception area. It fixed me with its glowing green eyes for a few seconds before closing them and dozing off. Monty returned in another suit and picked up his cup.

"Much better." Monty pulled on the sleeves of his new jacket.

Dex grew serious. "Are you sure you won't reconsider?"

"And wait for another Ghost tribus to pay me a visit?" Monty asked. "No, if Oliver wants to kill me, he's going to have to do it himself."

"That's what I'm afraid of," Dex answered. "At least let's get help."

"Whom do you propose?" Monty asked, wary. "None of your 'acquaintances' from the old country, thank you."

"LD Tush?" Dex asked, wincing.

"You're thinking of using the Ten?"

"No. Just LD…and maybe TK?"

"Are you mad?" Monty asked, shaking his head. "LD is the worst of the lot!"

"He's also the most dangerous and knows how to get in and out without getting us killed." Dex held up his hands in mock surrender. "I'll convince him to leave TK at the shop."

"Only if we want the Sanctuary standing when we're through," Monty shot back. "She's *twice* as dangerous as he is."

"It's decided, then!" Dex rubbed his hands. "I'll pack some things and we'll port over to the Tushes'."

Dex ran back into his room, leaving me completely confused.

"Who or what is an LD or TK? The Ten what?"

"The Tushes are, like my uncle, rogue mages that currently run an artifact business." Monty shook his head. "They are presently the only direct competition to the Moving Market."

"And this Ten?"

"During the war there was a covert group of renegade mages known as the Terrifying Ten. I don't know how many of them are still alive, outside LD, TK, and one or two others crazy enough to befriend my uncle."

"I didn't know the Moving Market had competition."

"Fordey Boutique is a very special kind of 'store.' The Market would never move against them," Monty said. "They tried—once."

"What do they sell?" I asked. "Are they as large as the market?"

"No, they would be considered a boutique shop

selling a very specific commodity," Monty said. "If the Moving Market is Selfridges, those two are Halimeh in Knightsbridge."

"And *what* do they sell?" I asked, concerned. "This sounds like a bad move."

"Death, destruction, devastation, and death," Monty said with a sigh. "This is going to be a nightmare."

"You said death twice."

Monty took a long sip of his tea and stared at me.

"I know."

TWO

WE MOVED TO the conference room, and Monty gently placed a long, slender case, on the table.

"How powerful is your father?" I asked, taking a seat.

"What type of power do you mean? He wields considerable influence as one of the Elders. Or do you mean raw power as a mage?"

"I mean mageosity, in relation to this Oliver person, who currently wants you erased and who managed to imprison your dad. How did that happen?"

Monty grabbed a coaster and placed the teacup on the table, looked off into the distance. "I don't know. My father is an Elder. Only Archmages are stronger than the Elders."

"So Oliver is an Archmage?"

"Impossible." Monty looked at me. "Oliver is powerful, but not *that* powerful."

"He's stronger than you?"

He sipped his tea again and stared past me. "Much stronger," he said quietly over the rim of the teacup. "Oliver Rank is older than my father, and one of the strongest Elders in the Golden Circle."

Fear did a little shimmy up and down my spine. I clamped down on it before it became a full-blown dance party.

"Can we send him a strongly-worded email? You know, 'no more mage hit-squads, and let my father go.' That sort of thing?"

He gave me a 'you can't possibly be that dense' look and shook his head. "Unfortunately, no. This has to be resolved face to face."

"If this Oliver isn't an Archmage, and he's not much stronger than your dad…"

"How did he manage to imprison him?" Monty finished.

"Exactly. It means this Oliver has leverage on your dad somehow. It's not you, since he's trying to actively keep you away by introducing you to the dirtnap club. Do you have any other siblings besides William? Could he be using them? What about your mother?"

Monty stiffened and looked away before speaking again.

"It wouldn't be William or my mother. We need to get on the grounds."

"How close is your dad to becoming an Archmage?"

"My father is one of the oldest and strongest Elders, even older than Uncle Dex. If I had to guess, I'd say two to three shifts away from achieving Archmage."

I rubbed my chin in thought. My brain had a hard time trying to grasp that level of power.

"When we visited, I noticed your dad wasn't being mistreated. His quarters, while small by Elder standards, were still comfortable."

"Now that I recall, he was more concerned for my safety than his own," Monty said. "He expressly warned me not to return. Why would he do that?"

"Because he knows how well you follow instructions?"

He gave me a quick glare and a scowl.

"No, it was the way he said it—'They can't hurt me, but they will kill you'—that sticks in my memory."

I sensed Peaches padding into the conference room and camping under the table.

<Are we getting more meat soon?>

"Is that all you think about? Do I look like a butcher?"

Monty gave me a puzzled look. "Not particularly. Sorry?"

I raised a hand and pointed down. "The black hole that is my hellhound would like more meat."

Monty raised an eyebrow as he opened the slender case, bathing the conference room in a deep violet light. "That is a surprise. I thought you had established a mental link with your creature. Or do you enjoy sounding deranged?"

"Old habit. Give me a second. I need to sort out my hellhound."

"Take your time," he said with a wave of his hand and focused on the case in front of him. He gestured, and a violet circle filled with runes materialized on the surface of the table. He produced a black cloth covered in symbols and placed it inside the circle.

Slowly and methodically he began removing items from the case. He made sure none of them touched as he placed them gingerly on the cloth.

Waves of runic energy washed over me as he arranged them on the table. They were black rectangular stones and looked like small blank dominos. I was getting a serious 'these things are dangerous' vibe from them.

My attention was diverted by Peaches, who gave me a hungry chuff, followed by a whine.

<Go track down Dex and see if he can make you some more meat.>

<He's in-between. Can we go to the place?>

"Can we swing by Ezra's on the way to get this LD and TK? What are those?"

"I'm not handling the teleport to Fordey Boutique, but I'm sure Uncle Dex can make an ample supply of meat for your hellhound."

I nodded and pointed at the small black stones that were producing black wisps of energy now. "Runic dominos? Because they feel like I should be running away screaming right now."

"Entropy stones," he said and glanced up at me. "You can feel them?"

I got up and took a step back, as the fear I'd clamped down on earlier began an Irish jig/salsa combo, accompanied by the little voice in my head advising me that Monty had lost his mind.

"My stomach is doing the hustle, and every fight-or-flight response I have is firmly set on *flight*. Why are you handling entropy stones, and are they as dangerous as they sound?"

"Fascinating," he said, staring at me. "I've never heard of a non-mage reacting to these stones. It may have something to do with your learning the

Incantation of Light."

"Wonderful, Mr. Spock. Why are you handling these things? For the record, the incantation doesn't work for me, unless you count that dried-up raisin of power that appears as an orb."

"Entropy stones are non-volatile, unlike entropy rounds. I'm giving half of them to LD and TK to see if they can help your creature with his problem."

"His *problem*? What, that all he thinks about is food and eating?"

"No, actually that's normal for the species. That and apparently utter destruction and devastation. No, I'm referring to his size issue."

I looked under the table, stared at Peaches, and shook my head.

"What size issue? He's under the table."

"Don't be daft, Simon," he said with a glare. "I'm referring to his transformation into a planet-devouring creature."

"Oh." I nodded slowly. "And entropy stones will do what? Shrink him? I thought the bond had to be broken for that to occur."

"LD and TK can use the stones to craft a collar for your creature that is attuned to your bond. You can control his transformation, if my theory is correct."

"And if it's not?"

"Then you unleash an unstoppable hellhound on the earth."

Dex walked into the room and glanced at the entropy stones. He whistled low and shook his head.

"Are you planning on erasing the Sanctuary?" he asked and stared hard at Monty. "Entropy stones are a little much, don't you think?"

"These are what I call insurance," Monty said, closing the case and leaving half the stones on the table. "Besides, these are for TK to form a collar for his hellhound," he added, nodding in my direction.

"Do you know how difficult it's going to be to fashion a collar for the pup? Not even Hephaestus has tried to do that. You think TK can?"

"I intend to ask her," Monty said.

THREE

"I DON'T SEE why this is so important," I said as Dex began to gesture. "It's not like he's going to go supersize on us again."

"Supersize?" Dex asked, looking up sharply. "What do you mean...supersize?"

Monty explained what had happened to Peaches in London, and Dex's face darkened.

"What's wrong? He's back to normal." I rubbed Peaches' head and scratched behind his ears.

Dex interrupted the casting and stepped over to Peaches, crouched down and brought his face level to the eager hellhound, who probably thought another sausage was going to materialize.

After a few seconds, Dex stood up and prodded me in the ribs with a finger. I jumped back in surprise from the sudden sharp pain.

"Clearly you're not dead," he said, rubbing his chin. "How did it happen?"

I rubbed my side. "Yeah, thanks for that scientific method of testing my vital signs. He was poisoned and

—"

"Poisoned? Nothing can poison a hellhound. They literally can eat anything… and usually do when transformed."

"The poison contained a magical component," Monty said. "We tried to prevent the creature's death, but we hastened its transformation in the process."

"And London is still standing. Incredible. How did you get the pup back to regular size?"

"Through our bond…I think. Not really sure, but I know it had to do with the bond, and pain."

Dex looked at Monty. "He needs a limiter. If not, any extreme trauma could trigger the change."

"Extreme trauma?" I asked. "Like what, not getting enough meat?"

Dex finished the circle. Its subtle green glow filled the room with its light.

"Like getting launched into the Thames by a deranged mage, or seeing you in imminent danger. The kind of situations that rarely happen around you two."

"And this TK can create a limiter?"

"It's never been done with a hellhound, but if anyone can do it, she can, especially with entropy stones." He placed a hand on my shoulder. "Before we go see them, I need to warn you."

"About?"

"LD is laid back and calm. TK can be a little…"

"Highly strung?" I volunteered.

"Lethal," Monty said. "Don't offend her. She's a creative mage."

"A what?" I asked, confused. "What does she create?"

Monty produced another case and placed the remaining stones in it. The second case was a deep burgundy and covered in runes.

"Reservoirs," Dex said while nodding. "Good choice, considering our destination. The Sanctuary will be shut down."

"She creates reservoirs?"

Monty looked at me and shook his head. "LD and TK are creative mages. It's a very rare discipline of magic. They're similar to wordweavers, except where wordweavers use the spoken word, the Tushes use gestures to create—or undo."

"She's not that bad. Stop trying to scare the lad," Dex said, and then looked at me and lowered his voice. "But you may want to mind your words around her. She's a trifle sensitive."

"A trifle sensitive?" Monty asked as he placed the cases in the teleportation circle side by side. "It took the Golden Circle several years to seal the crater she created when she lost her temper the last time."

"They provoked her, they should have known better," Dex answered and gestured, adding more symbols to the circle. These symbols turned and shifted as they materialized, while the other symbols remained static.

"Of course, being offered tea instead of coffee completely justifies unleashing a quantum vortex and almost destroying the Sanctuary across *every* time line. If it weren't for Professor Ziller, the Sanctuary would've been erased."

"She specifically stated she didn't drink tea. You don't drink coffee."

"I also don't try and destroy every establishment that makes the mistake of serving me the filtered liquid from ground-up beans."

"If she likes coffee then she has excellent taste." I tapped the flask in my jacket.

Monty narrowed his eyes at the circle. "Did you factor for the artifact's temporal shift?"

Dex shot Monty a look. "Of course I factored for the artifact. I'm the one who gave it to them, aren't I?"

"Which I still think was a bad idea," Monty argued, stepping into the circle and tugging on a sleeve. "That artifact needs to be contained."

"It's contained," Dex said with a mischievous smile. "Within the walls of Fordey Boutique."

I stepped into the circle, followed by Peaches and Dex. Herk flew in and landed on Dex's shoulder, and the circle flashed green as we shifted away.

FOUR

WE ARRIVED IN a large cramped shop. The marble floor was covered with boxes and crates of every size. On the walls, warped shelves that appeared on the verge of collapse strained under the weight of the items taking up every available inch of space.

There was a crash, followed by a loud noise and raised voices. A narrow aisle led to a large counter at the far end of the shop. I could see two people standing behind it, and they were arguing from what I could see of their body language.

Above us, a skylight provided indirect sunlight that filled the shop with a soft yellow glow. The entire shop was bathed in a magical ambience. I could feel the presence of power all around me. Most of it came from the shelves and inventory arranged around the shop, but a sharp spike in the energy level came from the direction of the man and woman at the counter.

"You don't get scared, you get angry," I heard the man say as we approached. He was average height, with salt-and-pepper hair and broad shoulders.

"Well, yeah," she answered. "Not even you, my love, are allowed to make me scream like a girl."

"Sounded close to a scream." The man put his hands on his hips and gave her a smirk with a nod, to which she rolled her eyes and sighed.

"Yodel like a woman, yes. Scream like a girl, no. But if you keep trying to sneak up on me, I promise you pain, and lots of it."

The man burst into laughter, followed shortly by the woman. They both turned our way as we stepped closer.

"We have company, hun," the man said, looking at us. "Lowercase, not like Attila. Boy, was he a pain."

She was tall, with long black hair. I could tell she trained physically from the economy of motion when she moved. I couldn't see what all the concern was, until I looked into her eyes.

Her green eyes took us in, and she smiled before taking a sip from a steaming cup of coffee. The smile stopping at her lips said welcome, but her eyes said 'piss me off and I will erase you.'

"LD, TK, good to see you whole!" Dex said, embracing them both.

"Dex, hombre! How the hell have you been?" LD asked, returning the embrace. "Come, let me show you our latest inventory. You're going to love this." He grabbed Dex by the arm, pulling him down one of the other aisles. TK stepped around the counter and looked at Peaches.

"Is that a hellhound?"

I nodded. "His name is Peaches."

<Do not bite the nice lady.>

<Do you think she has some meat? I'm hungry and we didn't go to the place.>

"Of course it is. Is he a pure-breed?"

"As far as I can tell," I said, holding my breath in case Peaches decided she was worth a bite. "He can be a little fixated on meat. I wouldn't get too close."

Monty glanced at me and subtly shook his head. I didn't know if it was to warn me, but I got the feeling TK wouldn't be the one in danger if Peaches decided to go on the rampage.

She gestured, and a large sausage formed in her hand. "Hellhounds are always hungry, aren't you?" she said, getting closer to Peaches and rubbing his head. "Eat this slowly and you won't be hungry for a good hour or two."

Peaches gently removed the sausage from her hand and proceeded to eat. As he was nearing the end, it would reform, creating an entire piece again. He parked himself in a corner to enjoy his magical re-appearing sausage.

"Thank you," I said, looking at the reintegrating sausage in wonder. "I could use one of those at home."

"I'll make sure to send one with you." She glanced over at Monty. "Hello, Tristan. You look well."

"Well met, TK." Monty picked up the two cases at his feet. "Did Uncle Dex inform you why we're here?"

She nodded. "Yes, he did, but first I would imagine you want to see the artifact."

"If you don't mind?"

"Of course not," she said with a small smile. "I understand your concern over its use. The least I can do is show you that its only purpose is to afford us some semblance of privacy."

She led the way down another narrow aisle. It led to what appeared to be a bank vault door. She made a motion with her hand, and the door swung open. The massive steel door, easily three feet deep, was covered with dark violet runes that pulsed in time with the throbbing in my head.

Behind the door lay a small, empty, steel room. The power flowing from the space felt like a vise around my head, which squeezed harder with each step as we approached.

We stood at the threshold and I looked inside. Runes covered every surface of the room. She gestured, and the power vibrating around us subsided from 'squeeze my brains to a pulp' to 'punch me in the gut' level as we stepped inside. The door closed silently behind us.

In a shallow depression in the center of the floor, surrounded by ancient symbols I didn't understand, sat a dark stone vibrating with power. I was simultaneously drawn to and repulsed by the stone. As I looked closer at the heart-sized gem, I noticed that it shimmered in and out of sight as it pulsed.

I could feel the energy of the stone enveloping us. Violet lines of power stretched out from the stone into all of the symbols around us. We were in a latticework of energy lines with the stone at its center.

Monty stepped close to the depression and narrowed his eyes. Pain squeezed the base of my neck, crawling up into my scalp as the dull throbbing of the room got worse. I rubbed my temples to try to alleviate some of the pain, but it didn't help. TK and Monty looked unbothered.

I leaned against the wall next to the door, barely able to remain upright. I felt like an elephant was slowly stepping on my chest, stomping me flat.

"Any temporal anomalies?" Monty asked. "The flow has been constant? No replicating events?"

"None. We keep it on a shifting cycle of planes. The stone facilitates the shifts, however we don't draw power directly from it but rather from the runes etched into the room," she said, pointing to the symbols all around us. "That is how we avoid a temporal paradox."

"What is that?" I managed between gasps as they both turned to face me. I must have looked like I felt, because TK gestured and opened the door, while Monty held my arm as he guided me out of the headache room.

"That is an artifact called the Black Heart." Monty looked at TK, who raised an eyebrow in his direction. "It bends time, and it's currently allowing Fordey Boutique to time-skip."

"Why does the boutique need to time-skip?" I asked as the feeling of being crushed subsided with each step I took away from the stone. "I thought you would want clientele?"

"Those who need to find us know how." She gestured, and the huge steel door closed behind us. I immediately felt better. "There are some who would attempt to acquire our items by force."

"So this is like the Moving Market? It shifts around from place to place?"

TK stopped walking and stared at me. She gave me a look, followed by a smile that froze the blood in my veins.

"We are *nothing* like the Moving Market," she said, the smile never leaving her face. "If you compare us to them again, I will test how immortal you really are. I'll be in the casting chamber, Tristan. If you'll excuse me."

She walked ahead and left us in the corridor. I saw Monty exhale as he glared at me.

"Is that polite, just leaving like that?" I asked. "At the very least, she could have escorted us to this casting chamber."

"The alternative would have been to scatter your atoms through this place," Monty snapped. "She was exhibiting monumental self-control by stepping away."

"Oh…yeah. In that case, she is a bit sensitive."

"I told you not to offend her."

"And how was I supposed to know that mentioning the Moving Market would offend her?"

"Assume that anything that escapes your brain and works its way out of your mouth will offend her, and act accordingly."

"Are you saying I shouldn't say anything? I'm not understanding the statement."

He sighed and pinched the bridge of his nose.

"I told you the Moving Market tried to move against them."

"Yes, you said it happened once."

"Nick tried to execute a hostile takeover of Fordey Boutique. He had the numbers and the firepower. He felt it was an easy target."

"What happened?"

"Instead of attacking Fordey directly, Nick kidnapped LD on an inventory delivery. He figured he would force TK to save her husband by giving up the boutique, thus achieving his goal with the least amount of violence."

"Sounds like a solid plan and a good strategy. She gets her husband back, he gets the boutique."

"There's a reason LD and TK are rogue mages. Nick didn't do his due diligence. TK is a woman of singular focus and determination. The first thing she did when she heard that Nick wanted Fordey was obliterate the boutique into rubble."

"But her husband?"

"Would be safe. She knew Nick wouldn't dare hurt LD, who is a formidable mage in his own right."

"So Nick just returned LD?"

"It was too late. Nick had dared to threaten her and take what was hers."

"Shit."

"Indeed." Monty nodded. "Destroying Fordey was her opening salvo. She then hunted down the Moving Market, destroying all of its nexus points until it could only appear in one place."

"Where?"

"Hellfire. And there she waited, while Nick plane-weaved everywhere without being able to open the Market. When he finally surfaced, she entered the Market and reduced rings eight, nine, and ten to nothing."

"She burned them down?"

"She undid them. When she was finished, it was as if they had never existed."

"Wait, but the Moving Market only has seven rings."

"And that is why the Market will never move against Fordey Boutique...again."

"Were those rings populated? Did she eliminate the people there, too?"

"Fortunately those rings were used for storage," Monty answered with a shake of his head. "Rumor has it that was how she restocked Fordey after its destruction."

"How did Nick survive that?"

"LD was able to stop her that day, but it was still touch and go. When TK gets angry, it's best not to be in her vicinity."

"Or on that continent," I added, shaking my head. "And we're bringing her along on this trip to the Sanctuary because…?"

"We aren't." Monty set his jaw. "I would prefer not to destroy my home, thank you. She possesses less restraint than I do."

"So she has none, because your idea of restraint is to destroy most of the building. You're saying she destroys it all?"

"Your attempts at humor never cease to entertain. Maybe if detecting falls through, you can join the circus with your creature. I hear they always need new talent."

"I don't know…she could be handy. I mean, it sounds like she went to the Montague School of Problem Solving. What's the tag line? 'Obliterate, then investigate'?"

Monty started walking away from me. "Let's go solve your hellhound situation before he becomes a huge pain… like the person he's bonded to."

"Ouch," I said, and ran to catch up.

FIVE

"YOU WANT ME to do what?"

"Create a transformation limiter, until Simon exhibits enough control over their bond to render it unnecessary."

"A collar? On a hellhound? Are you mad?"

"Yes... to the collar."

"I'm flattered you would think I'm capable of something this complex, but I don't think even Hephaestus would attempt something like this."

"What if you use Ziller's theorem of entropic instability? He posits that by surrounding an entity in flux with an entropic field, it can create an instance of stability with a window of control."

"You realize that, as a mage, Ziller was borderline psychotic?" she said, touching the side of her head. "Brilliant, but touched."

"His theorem is sound."

"For that, you would need pure entropic stones. Even I don't carry those," TK said with a shake of her head. "You'd need to go—"

Monty tapped the cases in his hand. He handed her the black case. She opened it, and her eyes widened slightly.

"Will those do?"

"Where did you get these?"

"The Hound gave them to me."

She narrowed her eyes at Monty. "You're playing a dangerous game, Tristan. I hope you know what you're doing. If this rebounds on me, on Fordey—you and I will have a problem. You do *not* want a problem with me."

"They were obtained free and clear without blood," Tristan said, matching her stare. "Can you do it?"

She looked down at the stones. "With these? Maybe. What do you have in that case?" She pointed at the second case, still unopened.

"I need magical reservoirs. The Sanctuary will be a null-zone, if I know Oliver. I need a way to bring access to magic."

"What shape do you want these reservoirs in?"

"Chainmail rings, to be discarded when the reservoirs are empty," he said and handed her the burgundy case. "Ten rings. Five stones as payment."

She looked up sharply. "Tristan!" She shook her head. "It's too much. One stone can pay for reservoirs and the limiter."

"I know. How soon until it's done?"

"I'll need a few days at least. The reservoirs are simple. I can assume you prefer amplification runes?"

"Yes, those would be best, considering the circumstances."

"I can't guarantee the limiter. What you're asking for

is a bond regulator for a hellhound. Outside of Hades, I don't think anyone can do that." She looked at me. "I'm going to need to explore their bond."

That didn't sound pleasant. "Why don't I like the sound of that?"

"Because it will be incredibly uncomfortable," she said. "I will have to delve into the bond and your innermost private selves. I doubt Peaches will have a problem with it. You, on the other hand, may have baggage."

"'Uncomfortable' I can deal with," I said. "I won't have a problem if it prevents a Planet Peaches. As long as it's not as bad as last time, I'm good."

"How bad was it last time?"

"Like driving ice picks into my ears with extreme force, followed by having all my fingernails ripped off with pliers, and chased with acid poured over open wounds."

TK nodded. "I see. At least I won't have to explain how excruciating the process will be."

"Wonderful."

"There's one more thing…" Monty said, looking at TK.

I glared at him, slowly shaking my head.

"I'm going to have my hands busy for a few days, Tristan. Anything else will have to wait."

"This isn't something you have to do. It's something I don't want you to do."

"Monty…" I started.

He held up a hand, and I shut up. If he was going to say what I thought he was going to say, I may as well enjoy my last few breaths before the end.

TK placed the cases gently on the table next to her, crossed her arms, and gazed at Monty. The temperature of the room dropped by about thirty degrees. Everything about her pose whispered sudden death.

"Very few people on the face of this earth can tell me what I can or can't do. Not even my dear husband, whom I love more than life, would presume to tell me what I can't do. Choose your next words carefully."

SIX

"THE SANCTUARY IS the only home I've known for a long time," Monty started.

"Let me stop you right there, Tristan. I'm incredibly fond of your uncle. In fact, Dex is like a brother to me. Outside of LD, he's the only person I would consider listening to."

"Then you'll understand when I say—"

"I wasn't finished." Her words sliced through the room, cutting the air into stillness.

The smile never left her face and then I realized where I had seen it before. A shark wears the same expression when it glides through the water in search of prey. TK was the equivalent of a landshark, except scarier.

"Please continue," Monty said after a pause. "My apologies."

I saw the thin sheen of sweat form across his forehead and realized the danger we had suddenly found ourselves navigating. It was very similar to walking in bear-infested woods and finding yourself lost, at night, and carrying twenty pounds of raw beef. The outlook was grim.

TK sighed and acknowledged his apology. I was looking for a way to slide closer to the exit.

"My fondness for your esteemed and slightly deranged uncle is the only reason I haven't lost my temper. I realize you and I haven't interacted much, Tristan. You were very young when Dex came into our lives, but make no mistake, my love for Dex notwithstanding, I will atomize you where you stand if you attempt to dictate to me what I should and shouldn't do, or where I can or cannot go."

Monty remained silent, and I knew what he was doing. I had seen him do it countless times. He was a mage who had faced dragons, ogres, and even a mad god. He was working out the possible outcomes of his next actions. This ability to pause in the middle of conflict and see several steps ahead made him a dangerous opponent. It was battle chess with life-or-death stakes.

"I think what he doesn't want you to do is make those reservoir rings pink," I said, cutting through the tension. "Not one of his favorite colors."

TK looked at me and raised an eyebrow. "Was this your concern, Tristan? Color matching?"

Monty nodded and gave a short cough. "If it would be no trouble, basic black is my preference."

"Always with the funeral look, these mages," I said with my most disarming smile. Guaranteed to calm them down and help them forget the moment they almost went thermonuclear on each other.

TK narrowed her eyes at me. "Are you in pain?"

"Not especially, no. Not that I would like to be," I added quickly.

"You have a good friend here, Tristan. I'll get to work on the limiter and reservoirs and inform you when they're ready."

She glided out of the casting chamber with the entropy stones. I let out a breath of relief and self-preservation.

"Are you insane?" I asked Monty as I turned to face him. "Were you seriously going to tell her she can't come…to her face?"

"It did cross my mind."

"Are you actively trying to get us killed? You told me not to offend her, and then you turn around and almost get us blasted into memories. Why?"

"My position remains unchanged." He pulled on a sleeve and looked away for a moment. "She's volatile, unpredictable, vulnerable, and lethal."

"What are you talking about?"

"Oliver isn't a fool. He'll see through her in a second."

"I'm not following." And I wasn't. From where I stood, TK sounded like the ultimate weapon. I was starting to think having her with us was a good idea when we encountered a castle full of mages intent on destroying us.

"You recall how I told you the Moving Market moved against Fordey?"

"Like I could forget."

"What was her weakness? How did Nick fail to exploit it?"

I took a moment to consider the story as Monty

began gesturing. He formed a large red circle on one of the tables that sat against the wall.

"Her temper?"

"Look past the temper."

"She destroyed Fordey when she discovered Nick wanted it. If I was Nick and I really wanted to stop her…"

Then it hit me. He saw my expression change and nodded as he kept gesturing. "Now you know why she can't come. If you were Oliver, how would you stop a creative mage with her amount of power?"

"I'd strip away the thing that drives her. The only thing she cares about. Then strike when she was distracted and vulnerable."

"Precisely, the one thing a mage must never do is lose control."

"But you can't be certain Oliver will use that strategy," I said. "He could use a different method."

He gave me a withering glare. "What would you do?"

Oliver was an accomplished mage. We didn't know what he wanted but he had managed to take over the Golden Circle. Shit, Monty was right. I would remove the opposition in the fastest, most efficient way possible. Everything pointed to one solution.

"I'd kill LD and then erase her when she was distracted, engulfed in her grief and anger." I hated the words as I said them, because I knew I was right.

SEVEN

"WHAT ARE YOU doing?" I asked as he kept gesturing and then removed a hair from his sleeve. It was a long black hair and I knew it belonged to TK.

He dropped the hair in the circle, and it transformed from black to red and back to black in the span of a few seconds.

"Creating a Smith Bridge keyed directly to TK."

"She's not going to like that." I shook my head. "You can pretty much guarantee your imminent crushing when you use that on her."

"We only need LD to get us in the Sanctuary," he said, gesturing as the circle vanished. "TK being there will be a liability. She places us all in danger, especially LD. He gets us in, Uncle Dex can then port him back, we free Father and confront Oliver."

"Have you discussed this with Dex? Because that plan sounds simple, which never happens to us. No plan survives contact with the enemy."

"Discussed what with me?" Dex asked from the other side of the room. "What did you say to TK? She's about ready to blast a hole in the wall."

My heart leaped and tried to pull an *Alien* move by bursting out of my chest. "He was going to tell her she couldn't come to the Sanctuary with us."

"Are you daft? She's not going to listen to you. She won't even listen to me, and I've saved her life more times than I can count."

"Will she listen to LD?" I asked. "Can he convince her to stay?"

Dex shook his head. "No one tells her what to do or when."

"Sounds familiar," Monty said, looking at Dex. "I created a reverse Smith Bridge keyed to TK."

Dex gave him a hard look.

"You're playing with forces you don't understand," Dex said quietly. "You can't lasso the sun, boy. Have you given thought to what happens after you use the bridge? You think she's going to stay here and what, knit a sweater?"

"I will not have her jeopardize this mission," Monty said with an edge. "You suggested LD. I told you how I felt about her. She's a risk and you know it."

"Aye, she's a bit hot-headed—" Dex began.

"She's a mage, a *creative* mage," Monty interrupted. "Hot-headed cannot be part of that equation. The bridge remains intact. The first sign of her losing control, I send her back."

"She won't like this. The bridge is a bad idea, nephew."

"I'm not particularly concerned with what she likes. She's volatile at the best of times. She could easily undo the entire Sanctuary."

Dex nodded and clenched his jaw. "Aye, lad, you're right. I don't like it, but you speak truth. If she finds out, she'll try to erase you for the attempt and me for being your uncle," he said with a mischievous grin.

The cold realization set in as Monty spoke. For all his destructive tendencies, I had never really seen him lose it. He had never gone on a rampage and lost control. If he was capable of massive destruction while maintaining control, I didn't want to think what could happen if he lost it.

"I'm guessing we aren't going to tell her, right?" I asked as they both stared at me. "What?"

"Only if you really want to find out how much death you can handle," Dex said and shook his head. "I wonder about you sometimes, lad."

"No. We aren't telling her, and hopefully I won't need to use the bridge," Monty said, looking at me. "Right now it's a failsafe if she behaves erratically while we're attempting to infiltrate the Sanctuary."

"Don't you think Oliver is expecting us? I mean, could it be a trap?"

Dex laughed and then grew serious. "I always think everything is a trap. It's why I'm still alive."

"I tasked TK with reservoirs and the limiter for Simon's creature," Monty said. "We need one more thing. A runic neutralizer."

Dex narrowed his eyes at Monty. "Are you planning on starting a war? No one keeps those around. Not even LD would be crazy enough to keep one here."

"I know where to get one," Monty said. "But I have to go see Steigh."

"Didn't she promise to kill you the next time you

met?"

"Well yes, but…"

"Wait, what?" I asked. "No one else sees a problem here?"

"Oh yes, nothing like having an ice mage angry at you for rebuffing her advances," Dex said with a chuckle. "They don't take rejection well."

I stared at Monty. "Are you serious? We're going to see an angry ex-girlfriend?"

Monty sighed. "She's not an ex-anything. We just had a small misunderstanding. I don't think she was serious about freezing my blood solid."

"X, that's a good letter to describe what's she's going to do to you two." Dex made an X sign with his fingers. "This is a bad idea, lad. Even if Steigh Cea weren't there, that place rests over a ley-line. Exposure to that much power is poison."

"Do we really need this neutrino thing?"

"I know I've been called odd and strange, but even I know better than to go see her," Dex said and crossed his arms over his chest. "The Stynes are dangerous. She must be mad now from living there. Besides, she won't give up the neutralizer willingly. This is too risky."

"Stynes?" I asked, glancing back and forth between the two. "What are Stynes?"

Dex grabbed my shoulder. "A Styne is a mage that taps directly into a ley-line. They use raw power. Except that it does something to them, twists their minds a bit. She'd just as easily freeze you as talk to you."

"It's a calculated risk. We need it if we're going to get out of the Sanctuary alive."

"I'm all for getting out of the Sanctuary alive," I said.

"Alive and in one piece is even better. Seeing an angry ex, not so much. Can't we find this neutralizer somewhere else? The Moving Mar—"

"Hush your mouth, boy!" Dex hissed, covering my mouth and glaring at Monty. "Didn't you tell him about TK and Nick?"

Monty waved Dex's words away. "I told him, but he likes living dangerously. To answer your question, only Steigh Cea Styne has a neutralizer. We *have* to go see her."

"But Dex just said she may be not in her right mind…"

"Bloody batty is what she is by now. Avoid her if you can, but once my nephew has set his mind, it's easier to move mountains."

Monty nodded and gestured as white runes floated from his fingers, opening a rift in front of us.

"This will get us close," he said while stepping through.

"Keep an eye on Peaches for me, Dex."

He gave me a smile. "You think you're leaving him behind, do you?"

"What do you mean?"

"You'll see. Stay away from that ice mage and don't waste time," Dex said, his face grim. "The whole place is dangerous."

I stepped through the rift, and the room disappeared.

EIGHT

THE FIRST THING that hit me was the cold. Monty stood a few feet away and appeared unbothered by the Arctic temperature. My breath formed small clouds on every exhalation. We stood in a large corridor with hallways branching off in every direction. Off in the distance, the main corridor opened up into a wide space.

We moved forward into the large space, which reminded me of a large skating rink. I could see stairs off to one side, carved out of the ice. In fact, everywhere I looked, it was ice. As I turned, I realized we were standing in some sort of atrium or main hall.

"You opened a rift to Hoth?"

"Keep your voice down," he hissed and began heading to another corridor. "When I said we were going to see Steigh, I didn't actually mean we were going to 'see' her."

"What are you talking about?" I asked, keeping my voice low. "You said she has the runic nebulizer and we need it."

"Neutralizer."

"You want to neutralize her? What the hell, Monty? Is she that dangerous?"

"No, she *has* the runic neutralizer, and we need to procure it. Preferably without her knowledge."

"Procure? You mean *steal*. We're here to steal this nebulizer thing? From a crazy ice-mage who can tap into a ley-line?"

"Borrow. She won't give it to us without a blood challenge."

"I'm not feeling great about taking this thing. Let's just do this blood challenge and get it that way."

"Do you know what a blood challenge is?"

"Do I want to know?"

"Not really, no. It's better if we just borrow it—trust me."

We entered one of the corridors. "Are you sure?"

"Once we return from the Sanctuary, we'll return the nebu—neutralizer."

"Why is it so cold in here?" My teeth were beginning to chatter as I looked around. "This place makes Siberia feel like a vacation getaway."

"You've heard the term 'ice queen,' yes?"

"Of course, who hasn't?"

"Stynes are a type of Jotnar. In this case, they thrive and dwell in the ice and cold."

"You mean like frost giants? You pissed off a frost giant?"

He shot me a look and continued.

"The Stynes aren't frost giants. They are decidedly female, and exceedingly beautiful."

"I'll take that as a compliment, mage," said the

melodious voice behind us. "Now, which one of you dies first?"

"You forgot to mention stealthy," I said under my breath.

We turned to face one of the most beautiful women I'd seen in my entire life. Sky-blue eyes blazed at me with thinly-veiled violence behind them. Her face was framed by white-blond hair.

The similarity to my landlord, Olga, made me pause. The woman towered above us and even had the same 'you are inferior' look as she peered down her nose at us.

"Hello, Steigh Cea," Monty said slowly. "You're looking well."

She narrowed her eyes at Monty and icicles fell off her shoulders as she approached. Her glare shifted from anger to murderous intent as recognition dawned. Behind that glare, there was a definite crazy dance going on. I almost reached for my mark, but Monty shook his head slightly.

"Tristan Montague, I promised I'd kill you the next time we met."

"I know we didn't part on the best of terms, but perhaps we can be mature adults about this and—"

I barely had time to register the large pieces of sharp ice slicing through the air as they buried themselves in the floor in front of where we stood with a staccato rhythm of promised death. I glanced over to see Monty standing very still as more shards floated in front of him.

"I think she's still pissed, Monty."

"What gave it away?"

I made sure my mala bead was accessible. She had moved so fast I didn't have time to activate the shield.

"Why are you here, *mage*?"

She said the last word with enough venom to make an Inland Taipan nod in admiration. The hate was strong in this one.

"I need the—"

"Have you come to fulfill the vow?" she interrupted.

"Steigh Cea, you need to stop overreact—" Monty started as I pressed the bead on the mala and shoved him down and out of the way as the shards intersected the space he had occupied.

We slid on our backsides out of the corridor and into the main atrium. My shield dropped as we skidded a few dozen feet across the ice.

"Were you about to tell her to stop overreacting?" I snapped as we got to our feet. "Are you trying to get us killed?"

"Her reaction is clearly disproportionate to the situation. I never agreed to the betrothal." He tugged on his sleeve as he stood and glared at her. "I fail to see why she's this upset."

"Betrothal?" I nearly yelled. "She's your fiancée?"

He gave me the 'you can't possibly be serious' look, scowled, and pointed to another corridor.

"It was a deception," he said, waving my words away and moving to the entrance of the corridor he indicated. "We needed to pretend we were engaged in order to execute a mission. It was a success, and we— rather, they—were celebrating. There was an excess of mead consumed and things became rather... exuberant."

"Exuberant? As in she really thought you were going through with it?"

He nodded. "This was over a century ago. Nothing was written, and it wasn't binding. I might add, I didn't agree to *anything*. It was all her sisters' idea."

"You *will* fulfill the vow or die." Her voice echoed through the atrium.

"She seems pretty bound. Wait, sisters…as in plural?"

Monty nodded and flexed his fingers. I drew Grim Whisper and Ebonsoul.

"She has five sisters, all as stable as she is," he said under his breath.

"Wonderful. This just keeps getting better."

"Steigh Cea, I need the runic neutralizer," Monty said as she appeared at the end of the corridor.

She smiled in response. It was the smile of the unhinged. I realized then that there would be no reasoning with her. We started backing up.

"How serious are the effects of the ley-line?"

"Enhanced magical ability, cognitive degeneration, usually accompanied by a psychotic break."

"How long before it starts to affect you?"

"We have twenty minutes on the outside, but that's a guess."

"Are these sisters of hers in the neighborhood? I'd really like to avoid a family reunion."

"It's in our best interests to do this with as much haste as possible."

"Will you fulfill the vow?" Her breath solidified as she spoke, causing ice particles to float to the ground.

"There is no vow," Monty said with a sigh. "There is

nothing to fulfill. You were all drunk that night."

"Then you die."

NINE

SHE RAISED HER arms and formed several ice orbs in each hand. They floated and rotated lazily above her palms. She stood in the center of the atrium, and I could see layers of ice forming on the floor around her.

"This isn't going to be a friendly snowball fight, is it?"

"Nothing about this is friendly."

We backed into another corridor, minimizing the chances of a rear shard attack. Monty traced the entrance with a finger and spoke a word I didn't understand. A thin wall of energy materialized, sealing the corridor.

Dozens of jagged, sharp, angry ice shards materialized around her, all pointing at us. Part of it was amazing. It was the fascination you experienced when seeing the crystals of a snowflake take form before your eyes. The less amazing part was when I realized she was making these shards to impale us.

"How is she managing to do all of this without, you know, finger wiggles or words or anything?"

"This place rests above a massive ley-line," Monty said, gesturing fast. "She can tap into the ambient energy of the line and reshape it. Remember when I said magic has a cost?"

I sheathed Ebonsoul but kept the mala bead accessible as I nodded. "Yes, use of magic requires energy, which is why you eat those wonderful-tasting dirt bars so often."

"That's the physical toll," he said. "There's a mental toll as well. Without my martial-arts practice and meditation, it would be a simple matter to lose control in the heat of battle."

He waved his hands in front of us. Golden trails chased his fingers as a sheer wall formed behind the first. With another gesture he reinforced the wall with a lattice of red energy.

"Don't think we need to worry about any kind of heat in here. Will that wall hold?"

"For now. Let's go."

He headed down the corridor away from the frozen mistress of doom. I looked back every few seconds as I followed.

"A century ago we would've been able to have a civil discourse about the matter." Monty stopped at an intersection of corridors, closed his eyes, and then turned right. "Her prolonged exposure to a ley-line has had adverse effects."

"Adverse effects, sure, like driving people bat-shit crazy?"

"She's not 'bat-shit crazy.' Perception shapes and determines one's reality." He pointed down another corridor. I didn't know how he navigated the corridors, but I guessed it was a mage thing.

"Her reality is that you two need to be together. She seems pretty clear about—"

A muffled explosion rocked the corridor. Small chunks of ice fell to the floor around us.

"That took less time than expected," Monty said, looking in the direction of the sound. "She must be using more of the line's power than I imagined."

I stared at Monty, who raised an eyebrow and did his best Spock.

"What did you think was going to happen? You thought the ice queen was just going to let it go?"

"Of course not." He picked up the pace, headed down the corridor to the left, and made a sharp right turn to face a large ice door. "The neutralizer is behind this door—and she's not a queen."

"That's what you're worried about right now? Her title?"

I felt the micro tremors race along the floor. They were quickly shifting from micro to angry-ice-woman-on-a-mission-to-stab-me-with-pointy-ice-blades.

"Jotnar are very specific about how they are perceived in most—"

"The door?" I yelled. "Can we just get this thing and get out of here?"

I emptied Grim Whisper's magazine into the ice door with no effect, and Monty just stared at me.

"This is what coffee consumption will do to you," he said calmly. "It's abundantly clear that that bean brew is fraying your nerves. If you'd try a soothing Earl Grey, you'd be able to remain calm in these situations."

I holstered Grim Whisper and stared at him.

He stepped to the side of the door and gestured, revealing a runic combination lock. He shifted the symbols around, and the door slid open. The room was bare, except for a small pedestal attached to the far wall. Sitting on the pedestal was a large ice crystal. It pulsed white, then blue, and hummed with power.

"Is that it?" I asked, looking around the room as I crossed the threshold. I felt a wave of energy wash over me. "That didn't feel right."

"Bollocks," Monty said under his breath as he shoved me forward. I turned in time to see him gesture as an enormous block of ice smashed sideways into him, sealing the entrance, and trapping me inside.

TEN

I STOOD VERY still.

I should have known the entrance would have been rigged with a failsafe. If I hadn't been in such a hurry, I would have stopped to check or, at least, mentioned it to Monty.

My brain was telling me that he was okay. I'd seen him gesture before under fire and come out fine. He had been gesturing as the massive block crashed into him.

I faced the oversized ice cube now blocking the doorway and heard footsteps. I moved back a few feet and listened. The steps stopped at the entrance.

"Simon," I heard Monty's muffled voice say, "you may want to step back."

"Monty, are you okay?"

"A little worse for wear. It would help move things along if you stepped back and to the side."

I took several steps back. "How far back?"

"Away from the direct line of the door will suffice."

I looked around and moved to the side. An orange

glow suffused the large block at the entrance. Seconds later, it exploded into the room, burying pieces of ice into the far wall.

I knew something was wrong the moment I saw his arm hanging limp by his side, bent at an unnatural angle.

"Monty, your arm…"

"Is broken," he said with a tight smile. "We don't have time to waste. Let's get the neutralizer before she unleashes more nastiness."

"I'm sorry, I should've seen that failsafe. It was careless—" I started.

He held up a hand. "We both missed it. I should've known the runic neutralizer would be protected somehow. Let's just get it and leave this place before—"

The wall with the pedestal and neutralizer exploded. I grabbed the mala bead and deflected most of the ice headed our way with the shield.

"Did she do this?" I asked as ice smashed into my arm, trying to pulpify it.

"No, this is worse. She must have tapped the ley-line extensively and caused a disruption in its flow. It's bleeding off energy to fill the vacuum."

"I only understood part of that, and it all sounded bad."

"Grab the neutralizer," he said as he gestured. "I'll cast a rift."

I managed to grab hold of the pulsing ice crystal as Monty cast a rift. White runes exploded with light, but no rift formed. The runes floated in the air, frozen. I ran back to where he stood.

"Are they broken?" I asked, looking at them closely.

"Why aren't they moving? Where's the rift?"

"I don't understand," he muttered under his breath. "The rift should have formed, unless…"

"Unless?"

"We need to go now, back to the main atrium."

"Isn't that back to Steigh Cea? The one who wants to make a pincushion out of us? Well…mostly you?"

"Can't be helped," he said. "It's the ley-line. Whatever she's done to it, it's compromised the integrity of the entire complex. This whole place is going to collapse at any moment."

"How about a regular teleportation circle?" I couldn't believe I was asking for gastric destruction. "Can you try that?"

He shook his head. "The line has created an inversion wave. That's why the rift runes didn't work. We have to leave the way we came in."

We ran down the corridors, retracing our path to the main atrium…and Steigh Cea. Cracks appeared in the walls and ceiling.

"Did she rig this place to implode once we tried to get the neutralizer?"

"No, whatever failsafe was in place around the neutralizer has set off a chain reaction. I doubt destruction of her home was the plan. This is a result of the siphoning from the line."

"I hope this neuralizer was worth it," I said as we skidded past one entrance and ran down another corridor. Up ahead I could see the open space of the main atrium.

"Neutralizer," he corrected. "Only if we want to leave the Sanctuary alive."

We arrived at the atrium, and in the center stood Steigh Cea. The smile she wore ratcheted up past insane and parked itself firmly in completely derangedville. She outstretched her arms when she saw Monty.

"You've come to fulfill the vow."

Monty nodded. "Find the rift," he said under his breath. "Fast." He turned to face Steigh Cea. "Yes, I've come to fulfill the vow."

She nodded and focused on him. The tremors going through the complex were getting stronger.

I turned around slowly in the atrium to orient myself. I was looking for the rift where we arrived when a nudge nearly sent me sprawling.

<Do you have meat?>

ELEVEN

"HELLHOUND!" STEIGH CEA screamed, as we all turned to look at Peaches.

Several things happened then.

I pressed the mala bead, creating my shield, as Monty —moving faster than I had ever seen—ran in my direction while he gestured. Steigh Cea unleashed a barrage of ice heading my way. Her screams echoed off the walls of the atrium.

Peaches dug into the floor as he faced her and growled. Runes flashed along the sides of his body and his eyes transformed into glowing red orbs. Normally his growls would be a welcome warning to whatever was trying to erase us. I saw him gather himself to unleash a bark.

"No, boy!" I reached out to grab him by the scruff, but I was too late. His bark raced through the space, drowning out everything, even Steigh Cea's screams. For a brief moment, everything was silent, a pause before the inevitable destruction.

I didn't know if it was because the bark had made me

temporarily deaf or if Peaches had mastered time control. I was going to go with the deafness from the hundred-decibel bark next to my ears.

The next second, sound and mayhem exploded around us. Cracking ice thundered above us as the ceiling collapsed. That was joined by the machine-gun pelting of ice smashing against my shield.

Monty unleashed a small army of superheated orbs, intercepting and destroying several of the ice spears as he joined us.

"I said look for the rift, not summon your creature." He unleashed a larger fire orb that disintegrated another group of spears mid-flight.

"I didn't summon him!" I angled the shield to stop more ice from impaling us. "He just popped up, looking for—"

"Let me guess, he was trying to solve Heisenberg's Uncertainty Principle and wanted your input?"

"No, he wanted meat," I said, staring at him.

"What a surprise," Monty said, glancing down at Peaches and then up at me. "Did you find the rift?"

"It's back there, just inside the corridor," I said as my shield dropped.

I pointed behind us as another part of the ceiling broke free and buried the entrance to the corridor holding the rift.

"You mean the corridor behind that mountain of ice and debris?"

I shook my head in disbelief and turned as Steigh Cea screamed again. The temperature of the atrium dropped even further. She focused on Peaches and approached us.

"You dare bring an infernal creature into my home?"

"His name is Peaches, not 'infernal creature'."

<Can you ask her if she has meat?>

<Are you serious?>

<I'm always serious when it comes to meat.>

I looked up as Peaches rumbled and bared his teeth. Black shards of ice formed and floated lazily in wide orbits around her body.

"Monty, that doesn't look good."

"Obsidian ice," he said under his breath. "Bloody hell."

"Why does obsidian ice sound like something we need to avoid?" I pressed the bead on my mala and nothing happened. "My shield is down. Shit."

"Obsidian ice carries a runic virus. Fatal to magic-users, although the repeated impaling may prove fatal to you as well."

"Well, that's reassuring. Can we not find out?"

Monty threw up a wall of golden light. The wall flickered and disappeared in areas, creating a barrier that resembled a golden wall of Swiss cheese instead of a barrier against dangerous black ice.

"This doesn't look very secure." I stuck my hand through one of the larger holes.

"It's the ley-line." He coughed in response. "It gives her strength, but it's draining mine."

He was looking a bit ragged, and I realized it wasn't just sapping his strength. The ley-line was affecting him.

"It's poisoning you." I looked around the atrium and drew Grim Whisper.

"You will all die now." Steigh Cea raised a hand and pointed. The ice raced at us. Monty gestured and formed a blue orb of flame. The heat from his hand melted the ice around him. He whispered something under his breath and unleashed the orb.

The orb burst through both the obsidian ice and Steigh Cea. The collision with the obsidian ice created a huge cloud of black mist that floated around us. The impact flung her back and smashed her into the far wall.

She crumpled to the ground and slumped against the wall. Monty collapsed to one knee next to me, coughing. She looked down at the large hole in her chest and gave a short laugh before spitting up a small amount of blood.

Monty got to his feet unsteadily and walked over to where she lay. I joined him a second later. For the first time, she appeared lucid. Her eyes were clear and lacked the deranged 'I need to kill you now' look.

"I'm sorry, Tristan."

"I know."

"It seems I've been near this ley-line too long. Did I try to kill you? My mind isn't what it used to be."

Monty gave her a tight smile and shook his head. "Nothing I couldn't handle. You should rest now."

"You need to leave this place. My sisters...they will come for you. Do you have the neutralizer?"

Monty nodded.

"Kept it safe all these years. Away from them."

"I know," he said with a sigh and began to gesture. "You kept it safe from everyone."

"Make it fast, please."

"I will." He nodded and gestured.

She turned her head and looked at me. "You're

running towards death. Keep those close to you safe."

I nodded, not knowing what she meant. Mages and their cryptic-speak.

"Step back, Simon," Monty said as he raised his arm. I moved back several feet as he created a glowing lattice of heat.

The blue-white lattice formed over Steigh Cea. He lowered his arm and the atrium filled with steam as it descended on her body. Seconds later, she was gone. He fell back as the steam cleared. I ran to his side.

"Casting around the ley-line may have been an error," he said. "My defenses have been severely compromised."

"We need to get out of here," I said, looking around frantically. "Maybe one of the other corridors?"

A low tremor crossed the floor and rumbled beneath us. Peaches entered pounce-and-shred mode and looked in the direction of the noise.

"Those would be…her sisters. Run, before they arrive," he said just before he lost consciousness.

"Shit." I looked around. The corridors would be a waste of time. Besides, I couldn't run around and carry Monty while looking for another exit.

Dex's words came back to me in a rush. *You think you're leaving him behind, do you?*

I turned to Peaches as the rumbling got louder, dislodging more of the ceiling above us. Large chunks of ice crashed to the ground.

<Hey, boy, do you know where Dex is right now?>

<The one who makes the magic meat?>

<Yes, the one who makes the magic meat. Do you know where he is?>

I tried to keep my thoughts as calm as possible as the impending doom of five angry sisters approached.

<Yes. He is with the nice lady and the other man.>

I really hoped he meant LD and TK. If not, this was potentially a frying-pan-to-fire situation. I grabbed Monty by the wrist and put my arm around Peaches' neck.

I figured that whatever method hellhounds used to travel didn't depend on ley-lines. This meant they couldn't be affected by inhibitors, at least not when it meant moving between locations. It was a guess, but it made sense since Peaches was able to find me.

Our lives depended on this guess.

<Can you take us to them?>

<Are we going to get meat?>

I shook my head in amazement at his singular focus.

<Promise. As soon as we get back, you get meat.>

He slobbered me with a huge lick, looked off into the distance as his eyes glowed red, and rumbled. The next second, the ice cave was gone.

TWELVE

WE ARRIVED AT the Fordey Boutique casting room with as much grace as a three-car collision. I crashed into a table, Monty rolled across the floor, still unconscious, and Peaches put a hole in the wall as he sailed into and through the room.

Dex and LD raced to where we lay sprawled out on the floor. TK appeared in the doorway a few seconds later, her hands covered in black energy.

"We have a breach," she said, and then she looked, expressionless, from the large Peaches-shaped hole in the wall to the floor where we lay. "Oh, nevermind."

LD looked up, shook his head, and made his way over to Monty. "We're good. No need to unleash the pain. They look like they've had a good dose of it already. His arm is broken."

"Did someone miss a teleport?" she asked as she stepped to the hole and looked through. "Wait, how did you get around our defenses if Tristan is unconscious?"

Dex looked questioningly at me, and I pointed slowly at Peaches. I moved slowly because every single cell in my body was screaming at that moment. This teleport took the pain of regular teleport to new heights, parked me between excruciating agony and mind-numbing pain, and left me there.

"The pup?" Dex asked in disbelief. "He brought you here?"

I nodded. The pain robbed me of my voice as tears streamed down the sides of my face.

"Ach, whose bright idea was that?" Dex shook his head and started to gesture. "He could've killed you all. He's too young to try a multiport."

"You mean I'm not dead? Because that's what it feels like," I said when I found my voice. "We didn't have a choice. Steigh Cea was gone and her sisters were on their way. I didn't think they were going to be open to having a conversation that didn't involve smashing us to little pieces."

"Steigh Cea is gone?" Dex asked quietly. "Did her sisters see you?"

"No, we left before they got to us."

"Think back carefully, boy. This is important." Dex placed a hand on my shoulder. "Did they see you?"

I took a moment to reflect, and shook my head. "No. The ceiling was caving in. Some of the corridors were blocked. No one was in the atrium when we left. They were still heading our way."

Dex let out a breath and visibly relaxed.

"That gives us some time." He moved over to where Monty lay, as Peaches padded over to me and licked my face. "If they didn't see you, we can hide your signatures before they realize Tristan was there."

<Feel better?>

<I keep telling you, your saliva doesn't have healing properties.>

<You look better already. Can you ask the old man for the magic meat?>

"What would happen if they saw us?" I moved to a sitting position as my body flushed with warmth and dealt with the effects of Peaches' teleport from hell.

"You wouldn't be here talking to me right now. What did they hit him with?"

"A huge ice block failsafe broke his arm, and I think he inhaled something called obsidian ice."

Dex cursed under his breath. "Did she cut him with the black ice?"

"No, there was a large, black mist, and he walked through it."

"Of all the pigheaded…. The neutralizer. Do you have it?" Dex asked with urgency. "Tell me you have it, boy."

I nodded and handed him the pulsing ice crystal. In the center, I could see the shadow of an object. Even though it was made of ice, it felt warm to the touch as it shifted from deep blue to bright white.

"Dex…you can't use it on him," LD said, his voice laced with concern. "You know the effects."

"He inhaled obsidian ice. Do you have a better idea?"

"I do." TK approached Monty's prone form. "Move."

Dex and LD stepped away from Monty, giving her space. She held out her hand and Dex gave her the crystal. The ice melted away, revealing a blue crystal about the size of a golf ball.

"What does that thing do?" I asked Dex. "Was it

important enough to risk his life?"

Dex clenched his jaw and gave me a short nod. "There are other ways to enter and exit the Sanctuary. Most of them are fatal. Even with LD helping us, it would be dicey."

"And this neutralizer makes it less dicey?" I looked at the crystal in TK's hands. It stopped pulsing and remained a deep blue. "What does it do?"

"Exactly what it's named for," LD answered. "It's a runic neutralizer. In the hands of a mage like Tristan, it can deactivate any rune or runic signature. He can't be touched by magic."

"Runic signature? Meaning you can't be tracked by magistrates or mages? Sounds like ultimate defense cloaking."

"Beyond that. It makes you invisible to any magical tracking…period." LD looked at TK. "But in her hands it's something else."

TK whispered some words under her breath, and the neutralizer floated above her palm. She removed her hand and the crystal remained in the air next to her as she focused on Monty.

"What are the effects?"

"LD, I may need you for this."

"I'll cast the support circle," he said as he approached her and began gesturing. A large gray runic circle formed under Monty. "You okay for removing the obsidian?"

"It's going to be harder because he inhaled it. But that's better than dealing with an obsidian ice wound. Let's tend to the arm first."

She rubbed her palms together. Black energy covered

them as she placed both hands on Monty's arm. The sound of ripping and tearing filled the room, followed by a subtle hiss. I looked over, and the arm was slightly swollen but intact. Black wisps of energy wafted up from his arm, reminding me of entropy rounds.

"You don't want to move him?" LD asked. "This may be safer in the workshop."

"No time. If that mist gets into his bloodstream I don't know if I'll be able to get it all." She narrowed her eyes and looked down at Monty. "We need to get it out now."

Dex put a hand on my shoulder. "There's a chance he could lose his ability to cast."

"What?" I stepped toward Monty. Dex clamped down on my shoulder with enough force to convince me otherwise. "You can't let her do this."

"We have to. Obsidian ice carries a runic virus fatal to mages. The only sliver of hope is that he inhaled it. If she doesn't remove it from his body, he'll be gone."

"Shit." I heard Peaches whine next to me as he lay flat on the floor and looked at Monty.

<The angry man is sick. Should I lick him?>

<He'll be okay, boy. Let's save your healing saliva for later.>

<I have a lot of it. I can help.>

<I'm sure if they need help you'll be the first one they call.>

<Can you ask the old man to make some magic meat? You promised.>

<Yes, I did, and thank you for bringing us back.>

He chuffed but didn't move from his spot, keeping his eyes focused on the unconscious form of Monty. I rubbed behind his ears and turned to Dex.

"Dex, I promised Peaches you would make him one

of your sausages if he brought us back in one piece.
Could you?"

"Meat for the pup? Of course."

He gestured, formed a sausage the size of my arm,
and placed it on the floor next to the black hole known
as Peaches.

"Thanks, Dex."

Peaches moved his head and gently placed his
enormous fangs around the sausage. He lifted it
effortlessly from the floor and padded over to the
corner. He turned around, so he could keep an eye on
Monty, and dropped his body down to the floor with a
thump. A few seconds later, he began to devour the
meat.

"Monty told me you learned the Incantation of
Light. Have you made progress? It's a good spell to
have in a pinch."

I looked over to where TK and LD were working on
Monty. I felt helpless knowing the process was beyond
me. TK's forehead was covered with a thin sheen of
perspiration as she peered at Monty, seeing something
beyond normal sight. LD kept gesturing as the gray
circle he created rotated slowly under Monty.

"What is she doing?"

"She's isolating and removing the virus from his
body, without leaving trace effects that would
permanently damage his casting ability."

"That sounds impossibly complicated."

"It is. If it were me, I'd just take him to the
Morrigan, but she's not known for having a deft touch.
She'd just as soon end his life and choose him. This is a
better solution, trust me."

"Will it work?" I said just above a whisper. "Can she do it?"

"I trust them with my life," he said, never taking his eyes off Monty. "And Tristan's. If anyone can do it, it's them."

TK gestured and motioned to LD with her head. They were operating with some kind of shorthand you witnessed when people were used to working together as a team. LD shifted to the side and made a different gesture. The circle went from gray to white. She nodded as the circle turned on its axis and bisected Monty's body at the waist.

"Ready?" The strain in her voice was clear, and I could see her jaw flexing. "I have it contained. I'm going to initiate the neutralizer and begin the expulsion."

"Will you be able to minimize the neutralizing?" LD asked. His gesturing was slower than TK's, but his fingers were moving faster than my eyes could track.

"He'll be comfortably numb for a short time. The obsidian didn't spread far." She turned to glare at Dex. "He should be able to create many more Smith Bridges in the future."

"Bloody hell," Dex muttered under his breath. "He meant nothing by it, TK. He thought he could—"

She glared at him again. "I believe that is a conversation Tristan and I should have, don't you think?"

Dex nodded. "Maybe giving him to the Morrigan would've been a better idea."

"She knew?"

LD gave us a tight smile and shook his head. "Your

nephew is a *pendejo*, Dex. Of course she knew."

"I told him it was a bad idea."

TK focused on Monty again and took a deep breath. I realized in that moment that if she were angry with Monty all she had to do was leave the obsidian mist inside his body. Why try to save him? Unless she wanted him healthy and healed so she could blast him to little Monty bits afterward.

"LD, I'm starting the expulsion. Slide the circle up."

LD shifted his gestures, and the white circle moved up on Monty's body, stopping at his sternum. "That's as close as I can get without displacing the obsidian."

"Good, that's perfect," she said and placed a hand on the neutralizer hanging in the air next to her head. The blue light filled the room, traveled down her arm, and flowed into Monty. "Keep it tight. We can't let this mist get away from us."

LD exhaled and nodded. He gestured, and the circle slid up slowly toward Monty's head. A black mist rose from Monty's chest, and the circle caught the particles, trapping them.

"Slow—I need to make sure we get it all."

LD kept gesturing as the circle slowed its rise, becoming darker with each second. After what seemed like hours, but was probably closer to only an hour, TK stepped back, handed LD the runic neutralizer, and nodded.

He gestured, and the circle turned on its axis again, a flat black disc, hovering over Monty's body. With another motion of his hand the circle transformed into an orb, enclosing the deadly mist.

"Bring it," Dex said, his voice hard.

LD and TK both looked at him.

"This is lethal, hombre." LD gestured, and the black orb was surrounded by several gray orbs each larger than the last, containing the mist in a Russian doll of orbs. "I thought this was a rescue mission. We use this, it becomes a massacre."

"Best to be prepared for every eventuality. I have an idea. We bring it."

"Sure, but this is bringing a nuke to a gunfight." LD shook his head as the orb floated in front of him. With another gesture, it vanished.

"Who said it was a gunfight? How long until my nephew can cast?"

"A day or two, three at the most," TK said, looking at me. "Plenty of time to work on the limiter for the hellhound, and the reservoirs."

"Good. I need to go see Mo about keeping Herk with her. The last time we were near the Sanctuary, it wasn't pretty," Dex said, running his hand through his hair. "She won't be pleased. I'll be back in a day or so."

"I don't know what you see in her, but it's your funeral," TK said. "I need to eat. That casting took it out of me. I'm going to have dinner and then get started on the reservoirs."

"TK…" Dex started.

"I know why he did it. I promise not to obliterate him, but he and I will have a *conversation*."

Dex winced. "Fair enough, woman. Just don't break him."

"I just fixed him." She waved him off. "Go talk to your insane goddess."

Dex formed a green circle and stepped into the

center. "Give me a day to convince her, and another to persuade her," he said with a grin. "I'll be back before she destroys my loins."

"Ugh, I don't want to hear about it, you dirty old man. Go."

Dex disappeared, and TK shook her head. "He's incorrigible, and crazy for being with her."

"Maybe he has a deep and abiding interest in pain?" LD mused, looking at the teleportation circle. "He always was a bit off."

"He must be to spend any time with her. Move Tristan to the guest room and prep him"—she motioned to me with her chin—"for the bond exploration. When he's ready, bring him to the workshop."

She left the casting room.

THIRTEEN

LD GESTURED, AND a gray circle formed under Monty. After a few seconds, his body was gone. My face must have held an expression of surprise because he clapped me on the shoulder and laughed.

"He's fine. I just moved him to one of our guest quarters. TK is going to speak to him about casting Smith Bridges on mages old enough to erase your ass. It will not be a pleasant conversation."

"I told him she would be pissed, but he's really concerned about his dad and the Golden Circle. This Oliver is serious about taking Monty out."

"Is he, though?" LD cocked his head to one side.

"What do you mean? He sent an Envoy, Arbiter, and then Magistrates. That seems pretty serious to me."

"And yet Tristan survived them all?"

"Well, we had help."

"Doesn't matter. If this Oliver really wanted Tristan dead, why not pay him a visit and end him right there?"

It was a good question. If Oliver was so powerful, why not finish the job himself?

"I don't know. Maybe he thinks Tristan is beneath him? Maybe he's one of these 'I don't get my hands dirty' types who delegates the killing to his minions?"

"You may want to find out the answer to that question. Something isn't connecting with this scenario. He can detain Connor Montague, who is easily more powerful than his son, but he sends lesser mages to deal with Tristan?"

"Those magistrates were pretty dangerous," I said, remembering how one melted the Goat. "I don't know if I'd call them lesser mages."

"The question still stands. What's stopping Oliver from finishing this job himself if he wants Tristan out of commission?"

"Is it possible he's not as strong as Monty thinks?"

"We'll find out. But first, we need to prepare you for a world of pain."

"Can you not sound so cheerful when you say that? What is this bond exploration thing?"

"Let me explain…no, we don't have time for all that. Let me sum up." He held up an index finger. "Follow me. Bring your hellhound."

LD headed out of the casting room. I crouched down and rubbed Peaches behind the ears.

<Let's go, boy.>

<Where is the angry man?>

<He's going to be okay. Come on, we have to find a way to make sure you don't go Lockjaw on us again.>

<What is a lockjaw?>

<It's a huge dog that—never mind. Do you remember when you became really big? We need to make sure that doesn't happen again.>

<Yes, the bad man gave me bad meat.>

<We're going to get something so we can control when you become big.>

<And then we're getting more meat? Do you know how to make the magic meat yet?>

<I'm working on it. Let's do this first, so you don't become huge again.>

"How is this 'bond-exploration' supposed to help?"

LD didn't answer as he led us down several dimly lit corridors. Most of them had shelving of some kind holding all sorts of items. At the end of one of these corridors, we came to another thick steel door.

This one was covered in black runes and gave off a 'run away now while you can' vibe. LD gestured, and the door swung open silently. It was easily four feet in thickness, making me wonder what this room was used for that required that kind of security.

"Does Fordey get vault doors on special?"

LD smiled, stepped in, and motioned for me to follow him. "We sometimes deal with unstable artifacts. Many of them are volatile and potentially fatal. This room keeps those effects contained in case of an accident. Oh, before I forget…"

He gestured and materialized a blue crystal. It floated in the palm of his hand.

"Isn't that the—?"

"The reason Tristan almost died? Yes. But we can't use it in here if we're going to activate your bond. It would interfere with the room. Give me a second."

As he gestured I observed the scorch marks and cracks in the walls. The far wall held a few craters in an odd sequence, and the ceiling was covered in jagged valleys. On the wall closest to me, I saw what appeared to be blast residue, and suddenly I felt less secure as the door closed behind us.

"Have you had many accidents?" I asked after the crystal disappeared. "It looks like a few have happened in here."

I rubbed a finger in the residue. I'd been around Monty long enough to recognize magical redecoration when I saw it. The room looked like it had hosted a mage battle royale.

"A few," he said with a chuckle. "But nothing too serious."

The room was about half the size of a typical high-school gymnasium. The wooden floors were surprisingly intact given the state of the rest of the room. Bright sunlight cascaded in from the large, thick, barred windows high up on one of the walls. The smell of old wood and lemon wax filled my lungs, transporting me back to my teens for a moment.

Power emanated from the room. It didn't try and crush my brain into jelly like the Black Heart room. This power was subtle and enveloped me. I turned, trying to find the source, but couldn't pinpoint it. The entire room was giving off waves of energy.

I noticed the subtle runes covering the walls and floors. Unlike a gym, there were no bleachers or basketball hoops. It was a large open space with only one entrance. I wondered how large Fordey Boutique really was. LD stepped to the center of the floor.

"In order to place a limiter on…Peaches, is it?"

I nodded. "Yes, Peaches." I looked around at the large empty room. "What exactly is this place? I've never felt a room with this much latent energy."

"I'll get to that in a second." LD held up a hand. "As I was saying, in order to place a limiter on Peaches, we need to evaluate the extent of your bond. How strong is it? How much control do you have over him? How well do you work together?"

"All this for a collar?"

He pointed at Peaches. "Is that a regular dog?"

"No." I looked down at Peaches, who nudged my leg and nearly dislocated my hip. "Far from it."

"Then all this for a limiter or collar, if that makes it easier for you to wrap your head around it, which will prevent your dog from growing to the size of a small bus and laying waste to an entire city, yes. Now, stand there and don't move until I tell you to. How do you fight?"

I opened my jacket to show him Grim Whisper and Ebonsoul. "Bullets and blade."

"Any magic?"

I thought back to the anemic Incantation of Light orb I created the last time I'd tried to use the spell.

"None worth mentioning."

"What about that mark?" He pointed at the endless knot on my hand. "What does that do?"

I had a feeling he already knew. "Stops time for ten seconds, occasionally gets the attention of Karma."

He nodded appreciatively. "Time stasis…nice. Gets the attention of who?"

"Karma—as in the embodiment of causality."

He looked at me in disbelief for a few seconds and cocked his head to one side. "An immortal who can stop time, is bonded to a hellhound, and can summon

Karma?"

"No, not summon. She doesn't like that term and she doesn't appear every time I use the mark."

"*She*? Really. I've never seen her, but last I heard, she could be a real—"

"Trust me. She is."

"Anything else? Do you transform into a dragon?"

"Nothing else," I answered with a slight edge. My last memory of dragons was unpleasant. It also reminded me of George Rott's call.

He stepped back about twenty feet and began to gesture. "I like to call this place the Danger Room. Usually I'm the one in danger when we're in here, so this will be a nice change of pace."

I stood still and could hear Peaches' raspy pant next to me.

<Is he going to make meat?>

<No, I think he's going to test us somehow.>

<By seeing how much meat we can eat? Can I have yours if you don't finish?>

"Do you want me to feel for the bond?"

"How long have you two been bondmates?"

I thought back to when I first met Peaches. It felt like a lifetime had passed since I first looked into the cage in Hades' office.

"Feels like forever."

"More than a year? Less than a year?"

"Less than a year. Definitely."

"Okay, that helps. Now I want you to sit down, close your eyes, and regulate your breathing. Feel for the bond and find the connection between the two of you."

I sat cross-legged on the wooden floor, closed my

eyes and slowed my breathing. I felt for the bond I
shared with my hellhound. After a few seconds, I felt
the tenuous strand of energy linking us. As I felt along
the conduit of the bond, it merged with another,
stronger strand of power.

I guessed this was my link to Kali. I didn't see any
way to untangle the two strands so I didn't attempt it. I
remembered Dahvina's words: *"Hellhound, Kali, and this
blade. You're thrice-bound, and two of your bonds are so
intertwined, I don't know if they can be separated."*

I let my senses expand, but I didn't reach for the
bond. If she felt it was too difficult to tackle the
entanglement, there was no way I was going to try it.
After a few more seconds, the flow of the bond slowly
solidified around my thoughts.

Peaches chuffed as he nudged my leg gently, nearly
knocking me on my back.

<This doesn't feel so good.>

<We'll go slow and if it gets too bad we'll stop.>

I placed a hand on Peaches' head and mentally
established the bond. A surge of power rushed through
my arm, but unlike London, this time I was ready for it.
It cascaded through my body, and I could feel the warm
flush of my curse dealing with the sudden onset of
energy. The smell of burned hair brushed past my nose.
I opened my eyes and saw the hairs on my forearm curl
up and turn to dust as they slowly combusted.

The surge ratcheted up a notch, and I grunted in
pain as LD kept gesturing. The power coursing through
my arm increased, and I felt the strain against my body.
If it got worse, it would be a repeat of London, and I
would have to try and survive an instant tan. Peaches

gave me a soft whine as the runes along his body grew brighter.

"Control the power." LD swept an arm horizontally in front of his body. The runes on the floor next to me became bright orange. "If you let too much in, it will cook you—literally."

After a few moments that felt like hours, I was able to reduce the flow of power from bathing in an active volcano to standing on an aluminum roof in hell. I let out a breath as the sweat poured down my face.

"Can you stand?"

"I'm barely forming coherent thoughts. Standing seems like over-achieving. How about fetal position?"

"Get up," he said with an edge. "You need to work this bond or your hellhound is a liability."

"Liability? He listens to me. He wouldn't go on a rampage. What do you mean 'work this bond'?"

"Listen, I know TK can be a bit abrupt and short-tempered, and if you tell her I said that, I'll deny it and roast you."

I stood unsteadily as Peaches started to rumble. I could see his muscles rippling as the power flowed through our bond.

<Easy, boy. He's a friend.>

"LD?" I glanced down at Peaches, who was incrementally growing. "I think—"

He held up a hand. "I'm not done. Tristan is worried about TK, and yet you two *locos* roam the streets of a populated city with a creature that's virtually impossible to kill and contains enough power to make a tactical nuke look like a firecracker."

"I think we may have a situa—"

"You have a handle on the bond?"

"I think so, but it looks like—"

"Good. Come at me."

I stood there, dumbfounded, for a few seconds.

"Excuse me?"

Peaches growled again and entered a pounce-and-maim stance.

"At least your hound is smart. He recognizes a threat when he sees one." He gestured and formed two white fireballs. They resembled mini suns floating next to him. With another gesture, an orange field descended over the entrance. When the door was fully covered, the floor runes became bright orange for a few seconds and then dimmed.

"What are you doing?"

"What are *you* doing?" he responded, gesturing again. Another white-hot orb formed in front of him, partially hiding his face. "We're heading into enemy territory."

"I know."

"Do you now? What do you bring to this fight? Attitude?"

"What are you talking about?"

"I count three mages with access to their power. Tristan is an unknown after the obsidian ice, which leaves Dex, TK, and me. You don't have or use magic."

I tapped my holster holding Grim Whisper and showed the sheath that held Ebonsoul. "I'm not defenseless. I can still do damage without magic."

"Really? You've got an overdeveloped sense of competence. It's going to get you in trouble one day."

He gestured with one hand while pushing in front of him with the other. The three orbs floated next to him.

I looked around, expecting an attack.

"That's it?" I asked, not impressed.

"That's all I needed. Did Dex tell you what kind of mages TK and I were?"

"He said something about you being creative mages."

"There are only a few of us because the discipline takes about a thousand years to reach the novice level."

"A thousand years?"

The realization that LD and TK were a minimum of a thousand years old caressed my brain and then squeezed.

He nodded. "Creating is difficult, and takes an insane amount of energy, but creating isn't the only thing a creative mage learns."

I reached down to unsheathe Ebonsoul, but it was gone. When I reflexively grabbed for Grim Whisper, it was also missing. I looked down and realized I was suddenly unarmed. Both of my weapons had disappeared.

"Leather holster and leather sheath, both unruned, unprotected, and easy to unmake."

He wiggled a few fingers at me with a smile.

"You destroyed my weapons?"

"Destroyed? No. I just relocated them. That blade is nearly impossible to unmake. And your gun is too sweet to destroy."

"Creative mages also can undo," I said, realizing the gap in my defense by not having runed my sheath or holster.

"Correct. That only takes a few decades to learn. Now you're unarmed with only your hellhound and your wits. What are you going to do? Glare me into submission?"

I was angry. Not at his words; he was right. I was angry at how easily he removed my weapons and how long it took me to realize the ploy.

"Fuck you."

"Oh, you're pissed now? Well now, I'm quaking. Is that how you're going to 'do some damage' at the Sanctuary? You're going to hurt their feelings?"

"I'm not entering this fight unarmed. I'll have my weapons when we get to the Sanctuary."

He shook his head. "You're still not getting it. The mages at the Sanctuary will have the entire compound shut down. That place will make Ellis Island look like a magical wonderland."

"So no one will have access to magic. I'll have the advantage."

He stared at me for a few seconds. "How have you managed to remain alive this long? Wait, don't answer that. It was a rhetorical question."

"If the Sanctuary is shut down, what's the problem? We use conventional weapons and get Monty's dad free."

"Except that the mages at the Sanctuary will have full access to their abilities." He let the words sit for a few seconds as the implications hit me.

"Well, shit."

"And lots of it. Then we have you running in, no magic, no weapons, and no clue. Classic redshirt maneuver: 'I wonder what this glowing mass is over here…maybe I should check it?' Poof. Dead redshirt."

"I'll just be a liability." I looked down at my empty hands. "I have no way to attack."

"You do," he said softly, as the orbs began to orbit around him.

"What?" I asked, looking at him. "You stripped my weapons, and my magic missile may as well be a spitball."

"You need to work the bond."

He raised a hand, and the orbs raced at me.

FOURTEEN

I PRESSED THE bead on my mala bracelet, and the shield materialized around my arm. I deflected the fireballs to the far wall where they added three more craters to the existing group.

"What are you doing?" I yelled.

He gestured, forming three more fireballs, and flung them at me.

"Work. The. Bond." Each word was punctuated with a fireball. He narrowed his eyes at me and smiled.

Peaches jumped and blinked out mid-jump. LD gestured and stepped to the side. Peaches blinked back in, and LD flicked a crackling gray orb at him. The orb intercepted Peaches and bounced him away from LD. Peaches flew across the floor and landed in a slide before hitting the wall with a thud. He shook it off, growing larger as he closed on LD with a loud rumble.

I slid forward, leading with the mala shield. Master Yat's words were coming back to me:

"If you rely solely on your weapon, magic or otherwise, you are a lame man using a crutch. A weapon is only as effective as its

wielder."

"So you're just as dangerous without your stick of agony?"

He tossed the stick to one side and hit me several times with an open palm before the stick hit the floor.

"That answer your question?"

"Yes. You have palms of agony too."

He extended an arm and the stick returned to his open hand. He swept a leg out from under me and assisted my swift crash onto the floor.

"You use the weapon. It does not use you. Now get up and run the drill again."

I felt for the bond connecting me to Peaches as he closed the distance to LD.

<Don't attack him straight on, boy. Come from behind.>

<Acknowledged, bondmate.>

Peaches blinked out again, and I stepped in with a vertical fist aimed at LD's chest. He twisted his body, causing me to miss, and unleashed another orb at me. It bounced off the shield and slammed into the ceiling.

Peaches reappeared behind him and pounced. LD bent forward, and Peaches sailed right over him and into my chest, knocking the air out of me. We rolled across the floor in a tangle, sliding for a few feet.

"Not bad," he said, forming three more orbs. "Are you done with cuddle time?"

I caught my breath as Peaches rolled to his feet. He was twice his normal size now, and the floor vibrated as he stepped forward.

<Stay close to me. When I tell you, blink out.>

<Are you referring to my phasing ability, bondmate?>

<Yes, when I tell you, phase out, return, and phase out again in rapid succession. Can you do that?>

<Yes, a rapid interphasing is within my capabilities.>

I ran at LD, who unleashed his orbs. Peaches kept pace by my side. When the orbs were a few feet away, I reached down and touched him.

<Now, boy!>

LD and the Danger Room disappeared. We reappeared a moment later to a perplexed looking LD, who fired another orb at us. The room disappeared again. We returned as LD shifted position, and I pressed my mark.

Everything grew out of focus as time slowed. I held my breath, expecting the heady smell of lotus blossoms filled with citrus and mixed with an enticing hint of cinnamon. This was usually followed by the sweet smell of wet earth after a hard rain, and a jaw-loosening face pat as Karma arrived to say hello.

I sighed in relief when she didn't appear. I closed in on LD. Peaches was mid-pounce as I swept LD's legs out from under him with a kick.

A few seconds later, the room snapped back into focus and the flow of time returned to normal. LD fell on his back as Peaches descended. He was done, or so I thought.

I was so fixated on LD's crushing by the hellhound that I dropped my guard. He noticed this and unleashed a barrage of angry crackling black orbs my way. Peaches blinked out again and reappeared in front of me. His momentum sent me spinning back as he caromed off my chest, causing the orbs to miss.

LD rolled to his feet as I slammed into the wall, gasping for air as my lungs burned. Peaches landed with all four paws on the wall and pushed off into a roll. He increased in size and landed upright with a crash, shattering parts of the wooden floor.

<ARE YOU INTACT, BONDMATE?>

"Oh, shit," I whispered under my breath, and winced against the sudden pain in my brain. "That's bad."

Peaches had grown larger than the London incident. He had passed small-bus size and had firmly entered large-truck territory. I don't know how many transformed hellhounds LD had faced in his past, but he remained composed, gesturing rapidly as Peaches stared at him.

<I'm good! Don't fry him with your omega beams. Also, can you try to lower the volume of your thoughts?>

<HE ATTEMPTED TO CAUSE YOU HARM. HE IS A THREAT AND MUST BE EXTERMINATED. FURTHERMORE, THOUGHTS DO NOT PRODUCE A VIBRATIONAL FREQUENCY THAT WOULD BE PERCEIVED AS SOUND.>

Wonderful, I was being corrected by Neil deGrasse Peaches.

<Do not go Dalek on him. He was just testing our bond.>

The orange field around the door disappeared as Peaches' eyes began to glow. LD swept his arms in front of him, and a light gray rune-covered orb enclosed him.

Runes materialized along Peaches' flank as he focused on LD. With a loud growl, his eyes grew bright, unleashing twin beams of red energy. They shot forth and blasted the orb around LD.

I managed to catch my breath and headed toward Peaches as the door to the Danger Room slammed open, cratering the wall next to the entrance. TK stepped into the room and calmly took in the scene.

"I clearly remember saying prep him for the bond exploration, not trigger the bond." She held what appeared to be a large necklace in one hand.

"I'd like to take this moment to confirm that their bond is quite strong, even though the hellhound is a pup. Look, he even has a baleful glare. I'm impressed."

"How do you suppose I get this around his neck now?" She lifted the necklace. "I fashioned it to the neck of a normal-sized hellhound. Not this hippopotamic landmass."

Peaches kept blasting LD's orb with his eye beams as he stomped closer. LD looked Peaches up and down from inside the orb.

"Yeah, he's pretty big."

TK sighed. "I just said that."

"Don't they get larger than this?" LD gestured, and another layer of energy appeared around the orb, reinforcing it. The omega beams bounced off the new layer of energy, cutting grooves in the ceiling. "Like, much larger?"

"Let's not find out." TK approached Peaches. She gestured and his beams disappeared. Peaches turned suddenly and faced TK. She crossed her arms and looked up at him. They remained that way for a few seconds, before Peaches wisely stepped back and chuffed. He didn't lower his head and maintained eye contact with TK.

<I CANNOT ENGAGE HER WITHOUT CONSIDERABLE DAMAGE TO THIS STRUCTURE, RESULTING IN HARM TO YOUR

PERSON. I WILL DESIST…FOR NOW.>

<Not engaging her is an excellent idea. Let's refrain from the engaging for now.>

"Thank you, dear," LD said. "I could have totally done that, you know."

"Of course you could have, darling."

LD gestured and the orb disappeared. Peaches blinked out and pounced, moving faster than any hellhound that size had a right to move. LD was faster.

He leaped to the side as Peaches reappeared, avoiding a massive paw that slammed down where he'd stood a second earlier, cratering the wooden floor. "I think he's still a bit upset."

Peaches rumbled as he circled around LD, who turned to make sure he was facing the oversized hellhound as they moved around the floor.

TK turned to me. "Simon, could you inform your hellhound that crushing my husband, while probably an incredibly satisfying and well-deserved act, is something I reserve the exclusive right to do."

I nodded. *<Don't crush him, boy. He was only trying to help us get stronger.>*

Peaches narrowed his eyes at LD and growled.

<HE IS A THREAT, BUT I WILL COMPLY. IF HE ATTACKS AGAIN I WILL RENDER HIM INTO COMPONENT PARTS.>

Peaches sat back on his haunches and sent tremors throughout the Danger Room floor.

"He says he'll stop trying to crush LD." I looked at LD. "If you attack again, he promises to bite parts off of you."

"My job here is done. No more attacks from me."

LD raised his hands in surrender as he stepped close to TK. "I knew you would be busy with the limiter and the reservoirs. I figured I'd trigger the bond and see the extent of the connection."

She shook her head. "I think you are the one with the deep and abiding interest in pain."

He turned to look at Peaches and me. "A few more decades, some training, and these two will be dangerous. I just nudged them on the path."

"How proactive of you. You realize if he had reached full size and phased, he could have upset the temporal stasis? Sent Fordey into schism and disrupted the timeline?"

"That's why I activated the floor runes. He grew at a controlled rate even though Captain Obvious over here was trying to warn me. I know, I know, my brilliance is blinding."

She glared at him, putting her hands on her hips. "Have I told you how dizzying your intellect is?"

LD raised an eyebrow. "I'm just getting started. They both managed to pull off multiphasing and effective thought transference...you can thank me later. He actually used a coordinated attack and made me almost get serious."

"Almost serious?" I said. "Those black orbs looked plenty serious."

"They were. If I half-assed it, your hellhound would have picked up on it. They operate on intent. My intent was to erase you."

"What if he hadn't pushed me out of the way? Those orbs would've—"

"Unmade you," he said, his voice hard. "I told you

we're heading into enemy territory. If you can't fight, then you're a redshirt. I don't fight alongside redshirts. They have a bad habit of spreading the dead to the group—no thanks."

TK sighed.

"Darling, could you see how Tristan is doing? I need to key the reservoirs to his energy signature, and I would prefer he be awake for that."

"Got it. I need to eat anyway. That little exercise managed to work out some of the kinks."

Little exercise? I looked around the Danger Room and understood why it looked like a war zone. In that moment, I realized Dex's friends were powerful and dangerous. It made sense after seeing Dex in action that he would surround himself with mages just as—or more—powerful as himself.

LD gave me and Peaches a quick nod, kissed TK on the cheek, and left the Danger Room. I looked on as he stepped past the threshold and closed the door behind him with a wave of his hand. TK stood quietly and observed me.

"You've managed to achieve thought transference?" She walked up to the massive sun-eclipsing Peaches and patted his flank. "Your bond is advanced for such a young hellhound. How did it happen?"

"We had an incident in London that kind of accelerated the process."

"I think I understand. Here."

She extended the arm holding the necklace.

"I thought *you* were going to put this on him?" I asked as I took it from her and held it up. The necklace was made of the entropy stones and was inscribed with glowing red runes I couldn't decipher. It vibrated in my hand and gave off a low hum as I examined it.

She gave me the 'you must be insane' look and shook her head. "I think you have me confused with another suicidal mage." She handed me a smaller bracelet, similar in design to the large necklace. "The small one is for you. Think of it as a physical representation of your bond. Put that one on first. Only you can place the limiter on him."

"You mentioned something about him becoming full size?" I looked up at Peaches, whose shoulder was easily a few inches above my six feet. "Does that mean he gets larger than this?"

"When he reaches adulthood," she said, looking at Peaches. "His transformed size will match that of an African elephant. There have been rumors of larger hellhounds, but those are reserved for his sire."

"Does this collar grow with him?" I held up the limiter and the hum grew louder. The sound reminded me of a hive of angry bees.

"It's called a limiter for a reason. Once you can control your bond, he won't need it. Put yours on first. I suggest the arm that doesn't contain the mark."

I put on the small bracelet. A surge of power raced up my arm. It felt like hitting my funny bone—with a sledgehammer. My arm grew rigid for a few seconds as the bracelet became tighter around my wrist. When I tried to remove it, I found that it was affixed to my skin. A jolt raced up my arm as I tried to remove it again, convincing me it was a bad idea.

"It's permanent?"

"When you grow strong enough to control the bond

without the limiter, you'll be able to remove it with ease. Now, you need to shrink your hellhound."

She crossed her arms and stepped back.

"Easier said than done. Are you here for the assist?"

She shook her head slowly and gave me a slight smile. "You misunderstand why I'm here."

"Why *are* you here?" I asked, focusing on the enormous infernal canine in front of me. I had an idea, but I wanted her to say it out loud.

"If for some reason you fail to revert your hound to a normal size, he breaks free of your bond, or worse, grows out of your control, whether figuratively or literally, my role is to prevent the massive destruction that would ensue."

"How? By locking us in here forever?"

"No, by reducing you both to ash."

"Oh, so no drastic measures. Good."

I glanced over to see if she was smiling.

She wasn't.

FIFTEEN

I SHOOK OUT my arms, took a deep breath and let it out. This was going to suck. Peaches sat and looked down at me. The industrial-sized version embraced the full effect of intimidation and fear.

The butterflies in my stomach crashed and burned as I looked up at him. He wasn't even at full size and all I wanted to do was run out of the room screaming. I stomped on the fear, remembering that this was my hellhound, no matter what size he reached.

I stepped closer, careful to avoid a slobber attack that could easily drown me where I stood. The runes along his flanks still pulsed with latent energy. Looking into his faintly glowing eyes only reminded me that I was in his direct line of fire.

I took another breath and released it slowly as I remembered the last time he was ginormous. I needed to reverse the process without the agony we went through in London.

<DO YOU HAVE MEAT? THIS FORM REQUIRES LARGE AMOUNTS OF

SUSTENANCE.>

<I can imagine. Before we get to the meat, we need to work on your size.>

<DO YOU REQUIRE I INCREASE MY MASS? I BELIEVE I CAN AUGMENT MY HEIGHT AND WEIGHT.>

<No! I mean, no, I don't need you to get larger. The opposite, actually.>

<YOU NEED ME TO REDUCE YOUR SIZE? THAT ABILITY IS UNKNOWN TO ME. I COULD USE MY EYE BEAMS, BUT THE PROCESS WOULD INCUR LARGE AMOUNTS OF PAIN FOLLOWED BY DEATH.>

<Not me, you. I need you to get smaller.>

He looked over at TK and chuffed. At normal size, this reaction let me know he's displeased about something. At planet-Peaches-size, his chuff managed to drench me in slobber and nearly knocked me off my feet.

I looked over and noticed that TK was slobber free, but she wore a small smile.

"I hear hellhound saliva has restorative properties. Judging from the amount of slobber you're wearing, you must feel completely rejuvenated."

I almost glared at her, but then my brain rushed me a memo reminding me that she shut down his omega beams with a gesture.

"I'm not rejuvenated, just covered in slobber, thanks."

<THE WOMAN POSSESSES ENOUGH POWER TO POSE A THREAT. YOU CANNOT ENGAGE HER ALONE.>

<We aren't engaging anyone. She's a friend.>

<SHE IS SPOOLING ENERGY WITH INTENT TO USE IT AGAINST ME. THIS IS NOT A FRIENDLY ACT.>

I remembered LD's words. Hellhounds read and operate on intent.

"Are you spooling energy?" I asked without taking my eyes off Peaches.

I felt the shift in energy around us as TK stepped back with narrowed eyes.

"Yes, I am. He's quite advanced for a pup."

"Could you not do that? It's making him nervous."

"You're standing in front of a seven-foot hellhound, telling me *he's* nervous about *my* spooling of energy."

"Yes, he thinks you want to use it against him."

"Who else would I use it against? Do you see any other hellhounds in here?"

"If you want him back to normal, I need you to stop spooling energy."

"Only if you can guarantee he will return to normal size. Can you do that?"

"He will return to normal size. On my life."

I reached out with the arm that wore the limiter.

<I ADVISE AGAINST THIS COURSE OF ACTION, BONDMATE. MY DIMINISHED SIZE WILL NOT PROVIDE AN ADEQUATE DETERRENT.>

<Trust me.>

He growled but remained motionless as I placed my hand on his head. A surge of power rushed through my arm and forced my eyes open. I grunted in pain and saw TK begin to gesture. I waved her down and she stopped.

The power coursing through my arm increased but, unlike the last time, I was able to direct the flow. My muscles were strained but they didn't feel like they were tearing themselves apart. The pain was worse than last time, and I really hoped that it wasn't correlated to his size. If it was, his full transformation would kill me.

Peaches' growl turned to a whine as the pain soared even higher on the 'melt my brain' scale. I collapsed to one knee as my vision tunneled in.

I clenched my jaw and ground my teeth as the sensation raced past my tolerance. The skin on my arm felt like it was being peeled off inch by inch, seasoned with sulfuric acid, and then sliced with red-hot razors. Warmth flushed my body as the curse tried to deal with the damage. I know at some point I started to scream. Part of my brain noticed the floor runes explode orange around us.

<THIS. IS. PAINFUL. SIMON.>

I could barely form a thought to answer him.

<We have to do this. Focus with me.>

A cloud of red energy flowed around us. His runes erupted with light. In the space of a few seconds, I sensed him getting smaller as the energy of our bond flowed between and around us.

<It's working, boy. We can do it.>

I reached over and placed the limiter around his neck. It adjusted to his body. The entropy stones turned bright red as another surge of energy blasted through my arm. I felt that familiar weightless sensation of being airborne. I landed hard and bounced across the floor, crashing into a far wall.

I lay on my back and took stock of the situation. TK stepped into my field of vision as a wet tongue slapped me across the face.

"I'm pleased I didn't have to end either of you."

"Me too," I managed after sitting up. "That wasn't fun."

<Do you feel better? You heard the lady. My saliva has destructive properties.>

<She said restorative, not destructive. Even though I think I'm agreeing with you on this one.>

<Can we get some meat? I'm hungry. More than usual.>

<Do you think I could recover first?>

I pushed him away before I drowned in slobber. "I'll get you meat in a second. Let me catch my breath."

TK gestured and formed a large sausage. She held it out to Peaches, who delicately removed it from her fingers and proceeded to devour it.

<You would recover faster if you let me lick you. Please say thank you to the scary lady.>

"He says thank you."

"He is quite the proper hellhound." She patted his head and rubbed his ears, miraculously keeping all of her fingers as he focused on the sausage. "The limiter will help you harness his abilities and strength. In time, he will become truly fearsome."

"In time?" I tried to get to my feet but the room swayed, suggesting that sitting would prevent me from introducing my face to the floor repeatedly. "What is he now? Because I'm not getting 'cute and cuddly' from anything that just happened."

"Right now, he's dangerous." She rubbed his flanks. "With the limiter—"

A tremor rocked the Danger Room, and I reflexively looked at Peaches. He looked up and rumbled, entering 'shred and crush' mode. I knew it was serious when he ignored the remaining piece of sausage.

<Bad men are here.>

"What the hell was that?" I leaned against the wall and got unsteadily to my feet. The curse was working to restore me back to normal. "Did LD explode something, like half of Fordey?"

Black energy covered TK's hands as she moved to the door.

"We have a breach."

SIXTEEN

I HAD TROUBLE keeping up with her as she raced down the corridors. We came to a T-junction, and I saw LD running toward us.

TK faced him as she began to gesture.

"The outer defenses have been triggered," LD said, biting the sandwich he held and groaning in approval.

TK turned at the sound. "Is it lean?"

"This is nice and lean. You make the best sandwiches."

"Thank you. Darling, when you were 'nudging' Simon and his hellhound earlier today, did you, by chance, happen to use a temporal spell?"

LD feigned insult and shook his head. "You know I would never use that type of spell when we're in stasis, dear. That would be reckless and put us all in danger."

"Precisely. That's why I asked."

"No," he said around a mouthful of sandwich. "He was the one messing around with time."

"Excuse me?" TK said, turning to face Peaches and me. She finished gesturing and a doorway opened in the center of the juncture wall. "The hellhound is otherworldly, but not enough to disrupt the time stasis."

"Not the pup, even though the phasing was a nice touch." LD pointed at me. "Him."

I looked behind me, because last I checked the only spell I knew produced a weak and sickly raisin of doom.

"I don't use magic," I said, shaking my head. "At least not very well. And I especially don't know any of these 'temporal spells' you're talking about."

We followed TK into the new corridor that opened in front of us. While the rest of Fordey was stone, marble, and subdued lighting, this corridor went in an entirely different direction. I could just as easily have been standing on the *Enterprise*. The door sealed the corridor silently as we stepped forward.

Fluorescent lighting illuminated the slick, hi-tech steel walls. The floors were made of some kind of polymer that felt like rubber matting. I could still see runes everywhere, but these were different from the ones in the other areas of the boutique.

"Just how large is Fordey?" I looked around the wide corridor in wonder as it branched off into the distance. "And what is this place, the NCC-1701 wing?"

LD smiled, finishing off his sandwich as he kept up with TK. "Fordey is as large or small as we need it to be. This area is the hub of Fordey. I call it the Kobayashi."

We entered a large room that resembled an operations center. Computers lined one side of the room over several long desks. The wall opposite the computers held large cases containing all kinds of weapons. A huge screen, bookended by massive doors, dominated the wall ahead of us. TK stepped up to the wall with the large screen embedded into the center of it. She placed a palm on a recessed panel next to the screen and it hummed to life.

The video split-screen measured about thirty feet across and was broken up into small rectangles, showing images of what I guessed was all of Fordey Boutique.

"Darling, explain it to me before I need to deal with our 'guests' in a manner unbecoming a lady."

"You've never been a lady, dear. Why start now?"

"Point taken. The temporal spell?"

She moved her hand across the screen and the rectangles slid across in the same direction.

"His mark"—LD pointed at my left hand—"creates a temporal pocket. I'd say about eight seconds long."

"Ten seconds, actually."

He nodded. "Ten seconds, sorry. I was a bit distracted during our bonding moment, trying to avoid getting chomped, mauled, and laser-beamed by your pup."

TK glanced at me and then back to the screen as she kept scrolling. "Is it a time-skip, or does it create a temporal anomaly?"

"From what I can tell," LD answered, "the flow is only disrupted for him, but he used it right after phasing with super-dog and that could have augmented its effect."

"Bloody hell," TK muttered. "And you didn't think to mention this to him?"

"I was nudging. There are no rules in nudging.

Besides, how was I supposed to know he would pull that move?"

"I sensed entropy orbs. What did you expect him to do, juggle them?"

"Dodge them or get dead. He dodged them with a sweet move, too."

"Is that how he avoided the orbs, using this pocket dimension?"

"No, he used rapid phasing and then pulled the move on me. One moment I'm standing there planning the eulogy, the next, I'm on my back with a few tons of hellhound about to land on my chest."

TK nodded. "Ten seconds would have been plenty of time for them to find us."

"There." LD pointed to one of the smaller screens. "What's with the masks?"

"Ghosts." TK tapped the small rectangle and spread her hands apart, widening the image. She narrowed her eyes at the screen. "Golden Circle sent a tribus, if I'm not mistaken. They aren't reading like normal Ghosts though, going by these energy signatures."

"Super Ghosts? Are they dark?" LD stepped closer to the screen. "They must've upgraded the training at the Sanctuary. These three are going to be difficult."

"They're not reading as dark. They seem to be gray mages."

"No way. Gray mages are a total pain in the ass. Are you sure?"

"Yes, this is going to be problematic."

Small black arcs jumped off her body, causing me to step back.

"Gray mages?"

LD nodded. "You have light mages, like Tristan and Dex, even though Dex blurs the lines sometimes. They use magic from the energy around them and spells they have studied. Then you have dark mages, who basically lean toward using life force—theirs or others'—to power their spells."

"And gray mages?"

"They're dangerous. They combine both methods, which gives them a huge pool of energy. Like an old diesel submarine. Once it runs out of fuel, it can switch to the batteries. Except in this case, the battery is life force."

"What are you?"

He looked at me before glancing at TK. "I don't conform to typical conventions of definition. I like to think of myself as a renaissance mage."

"You're certainly old enough," TK said, touching icons on the side of the screen. I saw doors begin to close all around the boutique. "Did you secure the Danger Room?"

"Yes. I think we may need to renovate the room after Simon and the pup. It took a real beating today."

"I'll make a note. Can you unsecure it? I'll send them in there and try to minimize the damage to the boutique."

LD gestured as gray runes floated around him. White trails followed his fingers as he finished the sequence. "Do you want it active or dormant?"

"Dormant, please. Thank you."

"Done. Can you leave most of it standing?"

"I'll do my best."

"One of these Ghosts melted my car. Can you

handle three?" I asked, concerned. "The ones in London were squashed by Nana, but she used something called the phoenix smash or something like that."

"You witnessed a phoenix fist?" LD said, the awe clear in his voice. "That is a beautiful move. Nana is the only mage I know who can pull that one off and live to talk about it."

"Nana, really?" TK turned to look at me with a slight smile. "How is she doing these days?"

"I can't believe they tangled with Nana." LD shook his head. "Those Ghosts were too dumb to live. Even I wouldn't mess with her."

"She didn't make it." The enso pendant she gave me still hung from my neck, its familiar weight reminding me of her warning about Monty going home.

"Really?" TK raised an eyebrow and turned back to the screen. I could see runes shift into place all over the boutique.

"Did you see a body?" LD asked, rummaging through a large chest in the corner of the room.

"What do you mean?"

"Did she expire before your eyes? Did you see her die, and watch her go down in front of you?"

"Well, no."

"Did anyone else? Tristan or Dex? Did anyone specifically say…'Nana's dead.' Was there a body?"

I thought back to the moment Monty and I went back to seal Nana's house. "Not that I can remember, no. But Dahvina agreed that she was gone."

"There's a big difference between mostly dead and all dead, you know." He finished rummaging and removed several large backpacks. "She may have left a large part of her essence behind to give the impression she died."

"I thought she was gone, from the way everyone was acting."

"I believe that was her intention." TK slid some icons down on one side of the screen. "Nana is usually reclusive. I'm sure Tristan had something to do with her surfacing."

"Yeah, she's gone. Not dead." LD chuckled. "Did she give you one of these?"

He reached into his shirt and pulled out an exact replica to the enso pendant I wore. His gave off a faint gray light. I reached under my shirt and showed him the one I wore.

"She said it's Tristan's."

He stepped close and touched it. "She made you his shieldbearer. He's not ready for it though. At least not yet. Maybe after another shift or two."

"So, she's not dead?"

"Nana is older than Dex, LD, and me," TK said without looking away from the screen. "To date, she has 'died' three—"

"Four, don't forget the explosion that wiped out that sect of Negomancers."

"You're right. She's been reported dead four times that we're aware of. I think she just goes on extended vacations and doesn't want to be disturbed."

"By faking her death?" I shook my head in disbelief. "Isn't that a bit extreme?"

"Not when you're as powerful as she is. Her abilities are quite in demand. Mages her age prefer to be left alone."

"And the pendants?" I tucked mine back in my shirt. "What are they for?"

"We can discuss those later." LD glanced at TK and held up the backpacks. "I'll get the bags ready, dear. Any preference?"

"Extended trip, heavy armor, please, darling."

"Serious?"

"Did it sound like I was making a joke?" The edge in her voice made me pause.

"No. It didn't." He opened his mouth to say something else and shook his head. "Just so we're on the same page, we are planning on leaving the Sanctuary intact after our visit?"

"That would depend on their response, now wouldn't it?"

"Extended and heavy, got it. Almost feel sorry for the Sanctuary."

"Will dealing with the tribus be too difficult?" I asked, looking at the screen. I thought I saw the pattern of what TK was doing. By activating certain runes, she was guiding them down the corridors.

LD stared at me for a second and then laughed. "No, I didn't mean difficult in the usual sense. I meant they aren't going to listen to TK's heartfelt pleas to exit the boutique."

I glanced over at TK. Her face was an unreadable mask. I could tell from her body language, and the small arcs of black energy that jumped off her every time she moved, that she was not pleased. She looked like a lethal human Tesla coil, and I took a few steps back to avoid being hit by a stray arc.

Peaches gave me a small whine and stepped back

too.

"Oliver isn't pulling any punches," LD said. "I retract my earlier statement about not getting the job done. These three aren't novices. Whatever he's doing, he's using heavy hitters. They're all yours, dear."

I looked at the screen and saw the three men walking down a corridor. They were dressed in black suits and wearing partial face masks that obscured the top half of their faces. From the way they moved, I could tell they were trained. Flashbacks of the melted Goat crossed my mind.

Their steps were measured and contained. At each corridor junction, one Ghost would look around the corner, while the other two formed orbs in case of an attack. None of them rushed, maintaining their triangle formation as they moved.

In addition to wielding magic, I noticed all three wore holsters and carried handcannons.

"People in masks can't be trusted. Oh, before I forget…" LD muttered as he moved to a container and handed me my weapons. Grim Whisper sat in a new black holster and Ebonsoul rested in a matching sheath. Both the holster and sheath were covered in faint gray runes. "This should prevent anyone from using the move I used on you."

"Did you secure the artifact room?" TK asked as she swept her hand across the screen and the headache room door appeared in one of the rectangles. Black wisps of energy crawled over the entrance. Just looking at the door began to give me a headache.

"It's locked down. Do we know how they found us? I mean, besides the temporal hiccup Simon caused. How did they know to look in this direction?"

"They must be tracking Tristan." She swept the screen again to a bedroom containing a sleeping Monty. "Secure him and begin the shutdown."

"They found us in London, too."

"They can potentially find him anywhere you go. They found us here when you used your mark. Along with the phasic shift caused by your hellhound, it must have disrupted the temporal stasis caused by the artifact."

"Do all mages speak this way?"

"Which way?" A look of momentary confusion crossed her face. "Oh, yes. I forget you're not a mage. Simply put, for ten seconds, as a result of using your mark and phasing with your hellhound, anyone with mid-level magical ability—like these Ghosts—could locate us."

"Uh, sorry?"

"Not your fault. How could you've known?" She glared at LD. "It's his fault."

"Even with the ten-second window, they would need his DNA to find him." LD expanded the rectangle holding the Ghosts again. "It's the only way they can track him anywhere."

"Who are we going to rescue at the Sanctuary?" She gave him a look.

"Shit, they're using Connor as a conduit."

"Precisely. Get the bags ready and collect Tristan. Once they're in the Danger Room, the boutique will be in lockdown." She pointed at me. "You and your hellhound are with me. LD, contact Dex. He'll have to cut his visit short."

LD gave a short laugh. "Oh, the Morrigan is going to love that."

"It can't be helped," TK answered. "Let's go greet our guests."

SEVENTEEN

IT TOOK US about ten minutes to arrive at the Danger Room. TK left the enormous door open behind us. The runes, which had blazed a bright orange along the floor earlier, were now dormant. The room looked like a large space used for controlled detonations.

"We'll try diplomacy first." She shook out her hands and flexed her fingers, cracking them with each fist she formed. "It's possible they'll listen to reason."

"Hasn't been my experience with Ghosts so far, but I guess there's always a first time."

I loosened Grim Whisper in the new holster and made sure I had access to Ebonsoul. Peaches bumped my leg, nearly shattering my knee.

<What?>

<Do you have any meat?>

<No, boy. We're about to speak to some bad men. Can you wait until we deal with this situation?>

<Can I bite them?>

<Stay back unless they threaten you. These men are

dangerous.>

The runes etched into the stones around his neck pulsed a faint red as he entered a pounce-and-crush mode.

<The bad men are coming.>

The tribus approached the Danger Room slowly. I sensed them down the corridor, now that all of the room's runes were dormant. Black arcs crisscrossed tightly around TK's body.

The three men entered the Danger Room with orbs of flame in their hands.

"We're here for Mage Tristan Montague. Hand him over," the lead Ghost said, "or suffer the consequences."

Something about the voice sounded familiar. Most likely the level of arrogance with which he demanded Monty, and the total lack of observation.

"Gideon?"

The lead Ghost stiffened. He extinguished the orb he held and turned to me. The two other Ghosts fanned out to either side, keeping the orbs in their hands.

"Where is he?" The center Ghost stepped forward.

"That *is* you. You're a Ghost now? Nice promotion."

"You know this Ghost?" TK asked, keeping her eyes fixed on the tribus.

I rested my hand on my holster, remembering how trigger-happy he was the last time he faced Monty. "Last time we met, he wasn't a Ghost, he was an Envoy. Monty shunted him back and put a hurting on him. He ended up in intensive care."

"I see you still have your helldog, Strong."

"How's the stomach? Back to solids, are we?"

Peaches growled at them from my side.

"Envoy to Ghost?" TK narrowed her eyes. "That is quite the promotion."

"By order of High Archmage Oliver Rank, Overseer of the Golden Circle, you are hereby instructed to surrender rogue mage Tristan Montague into our custody," Gideon said.

"Overseer of the Golden Circle?" TK raised an eyebrow and the black arcs around her increased in intensity. "I see you aren't the only one who has received a promotion. Since when does the Golden Circle have an 'overseer?' Where is the Tribunal?"

"Since the Tribunal was ineffective, outdated, and lacked vision, they were disbanded."

"I'm sure it was," I said. "Why do I get the feeling they were disbanded permanently?"

"They refused to comply and were incarcerated. Those who dared to retaliate were erased."

"Is that Oliver's plan?" TK cocked her head to one side and cracked her neck. "To erase Tristan?"

"I've been instructed to bring in Tristan Montague for a meeting with the High Archmage. He has matters he would like to discuss with him."

"This isn't about the void vortex?"

"I'm under no obligation to discuss anything with you, Strong. I advise that you and your malevolent mutt stay out of our way."

I was liking Gideon the Ghost less and less by the second.

"Peaches is a purebred hellhound, and you…you're an asshole."

TK looked around the Danger Room and spread her

arms. "As you can see, Tristan is not here."

"His energy signature is in this location. You *will* tell us where he is."

"And if I refuse?" TK asked, as the hairs on the back of my neck all stood on end. She hadn't moved, but the energy coming off her body made me step back. My first instinct was to run away. The voice in my head was agreeing, assuring me that it was the best course of action.

I ignored it and glanced quickly at TK. Her eyes gave off a subtle green glow, and she wore a smile that, for a second, made me agree with the voice. That smile was the promise of pain and death. She looked down at the floor, and I noticed the runes begin to glow.

"Then we are authorized to use deadly force to carry out our mandate." Gideon moved into a defensive stance and formed an orb of white flame. "Will you comply?"

"So much for diplomacy," I muttered under my breath as TK allowed black energy to cover her arms. I looked at Gideon and shook my head slowly. "You really don't want to do this."

"I said I'd try diplomacy, and so I shall," TK said with a sigh. "If you go back and tell Oliver to cease and desist from this course of action before we are forced to stop him, I'll allow you to leave here with your lives."

"Cease and desist?" Gideon sneered. "You'll allow? There are three of us. You overestimate your abilities, mage. "

"No, you just underestimate them," TK answered, her voice cold enough to cause frostbite in the Sahara. "I will not make this offer again."

"You think one rogue mage of questionable ability and some broken-down detective with a mutant dog pose a threat to us?" He scoffed and motioned to the Ghosts next to him. They spread out more but kept their triangle formation.

I made sure my mala bracelet was accessible. I could draw Grim Whisper in less than a second. Peaches was anxious to chomp on all three of them. Somehow, I doubted we would get the chance to do anything.

"No, Gideon. It's clear you don't understand the threat you're facing." I moved away from TK because I understood something Gideon and the Ghosts didn't.

Maybe it was the curse giving me immortality, or the times I'd sat down with Ezra. It could've been the many times I'd dealt with Karma or faced impending doom with Monty. In that precise moment, something became staggeringly clear: Gideon and the Ghosts were already dead. They just hadn't gotten the memo.

TK's eyes were glowing green now. Black energy swirled around her body. A mini tornado of destructive chaos churned up the wooden floor around her. TK looked up without raising her head and put her palms together in a form of prayer. A smile, almost gone but no less lethal, played on her lips.

"Say when."

EIGHTEEN

GIDEON UNLEASHED THE flame orb as he stepped forward, drawing his handcannon. The Ghosts beside him also released their orbs and followed Gideon's lead, drawing their guns as well. I pressed the bead on my mala bracelet and activated the shield.

<Can I bite them now?>

<Yes, chew but don't swallow. You don't know where they've been.>

Peaches took two bounds and blinked out. I rolled to the side and drew Grim Whisper. I took aim at the Ghost on the right. Peaches blinked in and bore down on the Ghost on the left. We were both too slow.

TK spread her hands and whispered something under her breath. The floor erupted orange as a wave of black energy engulfed the incoming orbs and slammed into the Ghosts. The two Ghosts flanking Gideon disintegrated into clouds of dust as the wave hit them.

Gideon managed to gesture and form a shield as his handcannon turned to dust. The shield lasted all of two seconds before it was undone. The wave coalesced into an orb and punched a hole through his chest, tossing him against the far wall.

I stood with my mouth open as I looked on in awe. TK dissipated the black energy around her and approached Gideon. I followed close, but not too close, in case she was still in a 'destroy everything that breathes' setting.

"You won't..." Gideon managed between gasps. Every breath was a wheeze and ended with a wet sound. He was bleeding internally, and I really didn't want to ask what spell she used on them. "...stop us."

Peaches nudged close to me.

<I like her, but she's really scary.>

<I agree. Let's give her some space.>

We both kept our distance as she knelt down next to Gideon.

"What does Oliver want?" She placed a hand on what was left of Gideon's chest. "What is he after?"

"What's rightfully his, ours: the world," he said, spitting up blood. "He will...unite all of the sects into...into one."

I was about to ask him how Oliver planned to do that, but TK closed his eyes as he stared off into space. He was gone. She stood and crossed to the entrance. She waited for me at the threshold.

Once we were past, she gestured and sealed the Danger Room behind us. Angry black runes covered the door. I didn't need to decipher them to know they were lethal.

"What was that spell? What did you do? You just unmade them."

"A negation wave," she said without turning as we headed down the corridor. "We must hurry. I don't think Oliver will stop sending Ghosts. For some reason, he wants Tristan. We need to get to the Sanctuary as soon as possible."

We headed down several corridors until I saw the familiar form of LD waiting for us near a large door.

"The Ghosts?"

"They refused to listen to reason. I even gave them an opportunity to return to Oliver...who seems to have plans of taking over the world."

"How does he plan on doing that?"

"Something about uniting the sects. The Ghost wasn't in the best of conditions to elaborate, but it didn't sound good."

"I have some bad news."

"The artifact?" TK said with urgency in her voice. "Did they reach it?"

LD held up a hand. "Artifact's fine. The room is sealed and still in stasis. No one can get in there. Except us."

"Where's Monty?" I looked at his face and his eyes were filled with sadness. "What happened?"

"He came out of the procedure intact. No internal damage thankfully and he's still in his right mind."

"But? Damn it, LD, just tell me."

"The fact that he inhaled the obsidian ice made it easier to contain and remove."

"The ice in mist form was too potent." TK put a hand on my shoulder. "I feared that might be the case."

"What are you talking about?" I reached for the door but LD held me back. "What are you doing?"

"Preparing you. He's not the same Tristan you remember. The obsidian ice has had some side effects."

"What are they? Is he hideously disfigured? Did he lose limbs?"

"It will feel like that for him. He can't cast or use magic."

"Shit." I pushed open the door and saw Monty standing against the far wall. He looked thin, frail, and older. If I looked closer, I could still see the mage beyond the years. I caught myself staring and stopped.

"That face you made...do I look that old to your young eyes?"

"No, of course not. You don't look a day over one hundred and fifty. Wait, did you just Jedi me?"

"Judging from your reaction, I must look how I feel," he said with half a smile. That reaction worried me more than the aging. Monty's face wasn't designed for smiling. Permanent scowl, yes. Smile, not so much.

"What happened?" I couldn't get over how old he appeared. "The mist aged you?"

"Not exactly. We can discuss it on the way."

"On the way where? The only place you look like you should be going is a retirement home. I hear assisted living is quite comfortable...they even wipe your bum."

"I may not be able to cast my own magic, but I can still use it." I noticed the thin bands of metal on each finger as he flexed his hands. "Don't make me scorch you where you stand."

TK raised an eyebrow at LD. "You gave him the reservoirs? But I didn't key them to his energy signature."

"I know. I did. He wasn't doing well even after I tried

a creative induction. I realized the obsidian ice blocked his access to magic. The reservoirs are keeping him alive."

"Wait, what happens when the reservoirs run out of magic?" I looked at Monty, concerned.

"If I don't have access to my magic by then, the Montague and Strong Detective Agency will need a shorter sign."

"We need to go." TK gestured and a door materialized in the wall opposite us. "Where is Dex?"

"He'll meet us at the airport. He almost sounded relieved when we spoke."

"I can imagine. I hear the Morrigan has a voracious appetite. Can you get my vehicle? We'll be right along. I need to have a word."

"Be delicate with the senior citizen." LD chuckled and glanced over at Monty, who glared at him. "You know how cranky they can get."

LD left as Monty skewered him with mental daggers.

"You tried to tether a Smith Bridge to my energy signature," TK said matter-of-factly with her hands on her waist. "That would have ended badly had you tried to use it."

"Yes." Monty straightened and stared into her eyes, which were thankfully not glowing green at the moment. "I felt you were a risk. I still feel that way but have realized that I may have been hasty in the execution of my concerns."

"Hasty is one word for it," she said. "Arrogant and foolish would be another way to describe it."

"You're volatile and vulnerable, TK."

"This is not news. I've chosen to have LD in my life,

and yes, that makes me vulnerable. What you call volatility I call decisiveness."

"Your *decisiveness* is why I felt you were a liability and attempted the Smith Bridge."

She looked over at me and nodded. "Tell me, Tristan. What if something were to happen to Dex, or Simon, or even Roxanne?"

Monty remained silent but looked away.

"You're more of a liability than I am. A megalomaniac is holding your father against his will. Your uncle makes me look stable and rational at times. Your closest friend is cursed by Kali, you seem to be allergic to intact buildings, and you're in love with a hunted sorceress."

"Hunted sorceress? Who's after Roxanne?"

"You haven't told him? And I'm the liability?"

"She's warded, as is Haven. No one and nothing can get close to her while I'm"—a fit of coughing interrupted his sentence — "alive."

"This brings me to your current state. You can't cast anything beyond what's in those rings"—she pointed at Monty's hands—"which means your usefulness is limited. In addition, you're aging at an accelerated rate. How much longer do you think you can function?"

"Long enough to see my father free and in his rightful place as an Elder," he answered, his voice as sharp as hers. "You will not prevent me from going to the Sanctuary."

"Oh no, we're going to the Sanctuary, and we're going to deal with Oliver. Once this situation is settled, and if you're still alive, you and I will have a reckoning."

"Understood," Monty said with a nod. "Your

conditions?"

"I've killed for less than what you attempted to do with your Smith Bridge," she answered quietly. "Because of the regard in which I hold your uncle… blood and power."

"No, no, not understood," I said. "You didn't see what she did. She put her hands together and then *whoosh*—deathwave. She took out three Ghosts in a few seconds…with one spell."

"Blood and power," Monty said, ignoring me. "*When* I get back from the Sanctuary… you will have your reckoning."

The throaty rumble of an engine cut through the tension. I looked outside and saw a 1970 Mercury Cougar Eliminator in glossy black and chrome waiting for us. The engine purred at me, and memories of the Goat rushed back.

"Our ride is here," she said, going outside.

Monty and I stepped outside into darkness. We stood in a large empty parking lot. When I turned back, Fordey Boutique was gone. "Where are we? What time is it?"

LD stepped out from the driver's side and opened the door. TK gestured, and the air shimmered behind us, closing whatever entrance existed. She stepped to the driver's side of the vehicle and got in.

"We're about five miles from Teterboro Airport." LD motioned for us to get inside as he held the door. Monty got in first, followed by me. Peaches, the sprawler, got in last.

"We're in Jersey?" I looked around the area but saw no landmarks to indicate where we were. "Fordey is in

Jersey?"

"Not really." LD closed the door behind him. "Fordey isn't really anywhere, and it's about five in the morning, give or take a few minutes. Ever since we installed the artifact, the boutique does some weird things to time."

"How long have we been in Fordey?"

"Time is an elastic thing in the boutique. It gets compressed and stretched. Have you ever heard of Ziller?"

"I'm familiar." I really wanted to head-butt Ziller at this point, because all he gave me were headaches. "Monty may have mentioned his theories a few times."

"Ziller has some excellent theories on Quantum Runic Compression. I have a copy of Ziller's laws of Quantum Entanglement."

"I heard that's a rare one." I was wary of jumping into this topic. Every time Ziller's name came up, mages went fanboy on me and started trying to melt my brain.

"It is," LD continued, the excitement creeping into his voice. "Anyway, entanglement posits that time is a fluid construct in which different quantum particles effectively share an existence, even though physically apart. Which means the quantum state of each particle can only be described relative to other entangled particles."

"So all mages *do* speak this way."

"Wait,"—he lifted a finger—"Ziller went a step further. He added imaginary runic time to the entanglement and uncovered Quantum Runic Compression."

"LD, he isn't a mage." TK glanced back at me

through the rear-view. "I doubt he's as excited as you are about this subject."

"I just wanted to know how much time we spent in the boutique compared to out here."

"Boutique time, maybe a day," LD said. "Real time, closer to a week. It's hard to tell without a comparative analysis."

"A week? Because of the artifact?"

LD nodded. "The effects of Fordey should help Tristan deal with the aging, since his body is still dealing with the environmental effects of being in proximity to the artifact in the boutique."

"And you thought I was bad," Monty said under his breath when I sat back, slightly dazed from the conversation. "Wait until you meet Ziller."

My attention was suddenly diverted when Peaches tried to muscle me over for some more backseat real estate. I shoved him back, forcing him to move two or three inches.

<You can't get the whole seat, so forget about it.>

He growled in response and sat half on the floor and half on the seat.

<What is wrong with the angry man? Is he sick?>

<Do you remember when you ate the bad meat that hurt you?>

<Yes, did he eat bad meat?>

<Something like that. He got too close to some bad air and it made him sick.>

<Sometimes after I eat meat, I make bad air. Is that what happened to the angry man?>

<Not really. He got too close to bad magic, but he will get better.>

The engine roared as TK stepped on the gas, basking in the rumble. She glanced over at LD as he strapped in and adjusted his seatbelt. We shot out of the parking lot and onto the highway.

"Who did you get to fly us over?" She adjusted the mirror and pressed her hand on the dashboard. Runes raced across the console as the engine settled into a low rumble. We raced along the highway, swerving around the minimal traffic.

"RJ is flying us over in a G650ERX."

"RJ agreed to this? We couldn't get Chris?"

"Chris is off somewhere, and RJ insisted. I'm psyched."

"If that's shorthand for psycho, then yes, I agree…I can't believe you said yes to RJ."

LD nodded and rummaged through the glove compartment.

"Yeah, can you believe it? This is going to be some flight."

"If by flight you mean hoping we don't collide with a mountain or any large body of water, then yes, it will be 'some flight.' I swear, RJ will be the death of me yet."

"Why aren't we flying out of a commercial airport?"

"No commercial flight goes near the Sanctuary portal," Monty said. "The only way to get near is a private flight, and a mage insane enough to go there."

"I'm guessing that rules out JFK."

Monty shook his head. "You plan on crating your hellhound?"

"I don't think they make titanium cages strong enough to hold him. Plus, all we need is for him to want a sausage midflight and blink into the passenger area looking for meat during dinner. That would go over well."

Monty looked out of the window for a moment, lost in thought. "Simon, I want you to do something for me."

"I'm not going to wipe your bum. I don't care how old you're getting. How old *are* you getting?"

"Without direct access to my magic, my age will catch up to me in about a week. Possibly longer with these reservoirs"—he looked at the black rings on his fingers—"and if I manage to reach my true age, you'll need a dustpan to have a conversation with me."

"Not a pleasant thought."

"Indeed. I need you to make sure my father gets out of the Sanctuary safely if we fail to stop Oliver."

I glanced up into the rear-view mirror and locked eyes with TK for a brief second.

"How about you make sure he gets out okay? Can we go with that as plan A?"

"Your word."

I looked into his aged face. His eyes burned with the same intensity I had always known, and I nodded.

"Your father will leave the Sanctuary safely if we don't stop Oliver."

"Thank you." He rested his head back and closed his eyes. "That makes this next part easier."

I looked forward and caught LD's attention. "Is this a SuNaTran vehicle? Reminds me of the Goat we lost."

"The Goat is a sweet ride." He nodded in appreciation. "The Eliminator"—he tapped the dashboard lovingly—"is TK's baby. It's not SuNaTran, even though Cecil is good people. His vehicles weren't strong enough for my TK."

"Not strong enough? His vehicles are tanks disguised as cars."

"I know, but TK can be rough on cars. This one can withstand both conventional and magical attacks."

"Our Goat was melted by a Ghost. He hit it with a black orb of nastiness and killed it."

LD nodded. "Sounds like an entropic dissolution. Did he hit it with a red orb first?"

"The red orb bounced us all over the place, then he slammed it with that black orb of destruction."

"The red orb acted like a runic neutralizer. It overwhelmed the defenses of your Goat. This allowed the black orb to destroy the vehicle."

"'Destroy' is a nice way of putting it. That orb melted the Goat."

"I've told Cecil that layering process has flaws but he won't listen to me," LD said with a shrug. "This baby"—he patted the dash again—"would've absorbed the entropic dissolution and given the coat a shine."

"Impossible," Monty said next to me with his eyes still closed. "The runic disabler stripped the Goat down to a normal car. There was no way it could have withstood the dissolution. The same would happen to this vehicle."

"Improbable, not impossible," LD corrected. "The Eliminator isn't covered in runes. They weren't placed after the fact. The runes are etched into the making of the metal. There's a reason Cecil moved to layering vehicles instead of using the metal infusion process. He tried it once."

"Is the infusion too difficult?" I looked over at

Monty, who had kept his eyes closed. "More expensive?"

"It limits the amount of drivers. Every car has to be keyed to an energy signature. I can only drive this one for short distances before it gets...irritable."

"The car is irritable...really? What's its name, Christine?"

He looked back at me, his expression serious. "When I say this is TK's car, I mean she's really the only one who can drive it."

"Cecil tried to improve LD's process once." TK looked in the rear-view and then shook her head. "It was a bad idea."

"He didn't follow my directions and tried to infuse the metal without the energy signatures being keyed." LD shook his head. "That was a disaster. Is that vehicle still around?"

"SuNaTran tried to destroy it, several times in fact, and failed spectacularly." TK swerved around a vehicle, headed for the exit, and entered the small airport. "Last time they tried, it exploded one of their shops. It won't take paint either...the thing is cursed. I don't know what Cecil did with it."

"Cursed," I said with a chuckle. "Cecil made a *cursed* car?"

"He did," LD answered, still serious. "But you'll never get him to admit it. He based it on a 1970 Chevy Camaro. Damn, it was sweet. SuNaTran modified the hell out of it. Armor plating, run-flat tires, and Lexan windows."

"Sounds like a tank."

"It made the Phantoms appear delicate, and that was

just the conventional modifications. The magical ones were insane. That entropic dissolution that melted your Goat would have bounced off this car without leaving a scratch. The last time we spoke, he was trying to find a way to unmake it."

"Three drivers?" TK asked. "Was that how many?"

"Yeah, three drivers died in that car. That's why Cecil called, to see if I could go over and disintegrate it. Everything he tried failed."

"What did you tell him?"

"I said no thank you. The runes he had used were ancient. They were cast in a way that would require a lot more firepower than I have…and I have a lot of firepower. I told him to dig a large hole, drop it in there, and seal it with cement and wards."

"So what happened to it? Did Cecil drop it into a volcano?"

"No, he did something scarier—he let the car find a driver."

"What do you mean he let the car find—?"

"We're here," TK said, ending the conversation.

NINETEEN

TK PULLED UP to a hangar with the number "20" painted on the side.

Inside, I saw what appeared to be a typical business plane. It was painted in light and dark gray shapes, which I realized was camouflage. I saw no designation numbers, except a large X on the tail. The engines on either side of the tail appeared to be oversized. I looked around and noticed that hangar 20 had no road leading to the runways.

Next to the plane stood three people. I recognized Dex right away. The other two, a man and a woman, I didn't know. They were both dressed in dark gray combat gear and gave off strong energy signatures. We got out of the Eliminator. Dex looked at Monty, frowned, and turned to LD.

"How long?"

"Two weeks, three on the outside if he keeps the reservoirs full. But he's your nephew, so we know that won't happen. The effect of the Black Heart is helping, but that will dissipate in a day or so."

"And the ice?"

"We got it all but it had already done the damage. It's possible he'll get full use of his magical ability back. We did all we could do. Now it's up to his body's recovery."

Peaches got out, stretched his legs, and yawned.

<Next time, I'm not sharing my seat. My legs hurt.>

<Stop complaining. Back seats are not designated hellhound accommodations.>

<They should be. Can you get some magic meat? When will you learn to make some?>

<I have other things on my to-do list that are more important than meat right now, but I'll ask Dex.>

<More important than meat? What is more important than meat?>

I shook my head and approached Dex. TK had moved to speak to the two people I didn't know, and LD escorted Monty onto the plane.

I patted my jacket and felt for the flask. "Do you think the Valhalla Java could help Monty?"

Dex placed a hand over mine. "If the runic neutralizer didn't restore him, the liquid in that flask won't help. This is more mental than physical at this point."

"I don't understand. Monty is a fighter. You're saying that he doesn't want to get better?"

"This is going to be a battle on several fronts, lad," Dex said quietly. "Going home is never easy."

Peaches nudged me, and Dex noticed. He looked down, smiled, and gestured. A large sausage formed in front of Peaches, who proceeded to munch on the meat.

"I'm going to have to learn how to do that at some

point." I looked down at my insatiable, bottomless pit of a hellhound.

"When we get back, I'll walk you through the spell." Dex shook his head and kept looking at Peaches. "After we deal with the Sanctuary."

"Thank you. I don't see how going home is making it harder for Monty to get well. I know he wants to get better."

"He's going to face some hard truths, truths he's been avoiding most of his life. Most of them unpleasant."

"What truths?"

"Let me introduce you to the crew." Dex grabbed me by the arm and led me to the plane.

"Which one is RJ? What is it with the initials?"

We walked over to the man and woman TK was speaking with. As we approached, TK stepped away, gestured at the Eliminator, and boarded the plane. I heard the familiar clang and thunks of the vehicle locking. A black wave of energy enveloped the car and then faded.

"This is RJ." Dex pointed with his chin at the pair. He motioned to me with a hand. "This here is Simon Strong, bondmate to the hellhound you see over there devouring the sausage, and close friend to Tristan."

"This is Kali's chosen?" The woman sized me up and pushed her glasses back up the bridge of her nose. Her reddish-brown hair was loose under her baseball cap. "I don't sense any magic from him. How did he bond with a hellhound?"

"René, be polite. It's clear he's having a moment." The man was average height and spoke with a slight accent. His energy signature was as strong as René's, and I guessed they were both mages. His black hair was cut short, and he wore a cap similar to hers.

"I don't do polite," she said. "When have I ever done polite? I'm being civil, aren't I? Haven't even had coffee yet, and here I am being civil. I call that a miracle."

The man extended a hand with a nod. "I'm Jonno, and this is René."

"I thought RJ was one person, like LD or TK? Do *they* have actual names?"

Jonno stepped closer and spoke quietly. "If they do, no one knows them. They've been LD and TK for as long as I've known them. Maybe Dex knows."

Dex just stared off into the distance. "Don't ask me. I don't know."

"You are a terrible liar." I glanced at him and turned back to Jonno. "Are you the pilot?"

"Co-pilot." He looked over at René. "The Strix is her baby. We'll be dropping you off at the Sanctuary portal, or as close as possible without getting shot down. It's been pretty dicey in that neighborhood."

I shook Jonno's hand, and René tipped her cap. "Right, then." She looked me over again. "Let's get this sorted. I only have one rule: Do not jeopardize the integrity of my bird. If you do, you'll find yourself freefalling from thirty thousand feet. This goes for you and your hellhound. If he cuts loose while we're airborne, you're off the plane. We clear?"

"Perfectly."

"Good, I need some coffee. I'd like to beat the sun, so take off is in ten. Jonno, I'll start pre-flight. Get me some coffee or so help me, I will not be responsible for my actions."

She climbed the stairs and headed into the plane, cursing under her breath.

Jonno looked at me apologetically. "She can be a bit abrasive, but she's the best pilot in the Ten."

"She's the only pilot in the Ten," Dex added and headed for the stairs. "At least the only one who will fly into the anomaly."

"Truth," Jonno said with a smile. "I'd better get her coffee before—"

"Jonno! Coffee!" boomed René's voice from inside the plane.

Jonno headed to the door on the other side of the hangar with a nod of his head. "Be right back."

"Where exactly is she flying us?" I climbed the stairs behind Dex as the engines whirred to life. "I noticed there's no road to the runways."

"About three hundred kilometers off the coast of Brazil is an island that serves as a nexus. It doesn't exist on any map. The portal to the Sanctuary is on that island, and we're going to try and land there."

"And this is difficult because…?"

Peaches nudged around me and settled on the floor near Monty with a thump.

"The runic interference around the island prevents any type of teleportation. Many have tried, but there have only been three people I know who've managed to land an aircraft on the nexus. Two of them are the pilots of this plane."

"And everyone else?"

"Vaporized on approach." He settled into a seat and fastened his seatbelt. "You'd better sit down before

René takes off."

TWENTY

"JONNO! I SWEAR, I will leave your sorry ass if you don't get here with my—"

Jonno poked his head through the doorway with a smile.

"Coffee? Did someone ask for coffee?"

"You barely averted your imminent death."

I saw that he had extra cups and handed Dex and me one before disappearing into the cockpit. LD and TK were sitting near the rear, speaking to each other in hushed voices. I saw the tension in TK's face as she sat in her seat.

She was sitting rigid and choking the handrests as black arcs of energy danced around her. LD was speaking to her in a calm tone. She didn't look at him as she responded.

"TK doesn't like flying, usually." Dex sipped his coffee. "She really hates flying with René."

"Because she's a suicidal maniac, that's why," TK said from the back. "I don't enjoy the sensation of impending death, unless I'm the one causing it."

"I heard that!" René answered and slammed the cockpit door shut. A few seconds later, her voice came over the intercom. "This is your captain, the suicidal maniac, advising you to fasten your seatbelts. We will take off in two minutes."

The Strix rolled out and taxied far enough from the hangar for the tail to clear it. I looked out the window and wondered how we were going to take off, since Teterboro Airport only had two runways, and we weren't anywhere near them.

I felt the plane lurch back as we lifted off the ground. I looked at the turbines and realized the Strix was a VTOL aircraft, equipped for vertical take-off and landing.

We hovered over the ground for a few seconds before shooting straight up. My stomach sank to the floor. I glanced back and saw TK's eyes glowing bright green. LD was still speaking to her. Dex was sipping his coffee. Monty was asleep with Peaches by his feet.

The turbines turned, and we started moving forward quickly. This only seemed to agitate TK more, since the glow from the rear of the plane intensified.

Jonno stepped out from the cockpit and sat in the seat opposite Dex.

"Runic interference near the nexus is off the charts." Jonno took a sip from his coffee. "We're flying nap-of-the-earth to avoid detection, but that means we have to stay under Mach one."

"I didn't think a plane this size could hit any Mach speed."

"The Strix isn't supposed to be a VTOL either," Jonno replied. "Dex, the problem will be landing at the nexus. We're going to have to go in dark. Which is going to piss off TK to no end. Can you keep an eye on her?"

"I'll do what I can. Tell René to make it as smooth as possible. How long before we arrive?"

"A few hours at our present velocity." He looked over at Monty. "Is he going to be okay? He's not looking well."

"I'll be fine," Monty answered, keeping his eyes closed. "I've been advised to conserve as much energy as possible."

"Sounds like a solid plan." Jonno nodded and raised an eyebrow. "One more thing. LD told us this was one way. How are you getting back? You can't stay on the nexus for more than an hour before the runic activity fries all of you."

"We're all going through the nexus, but LD and TK will hold the breach at the Sanctuary wall until we finish inside." Dex locked eyes with Jonno for a few seconds. "Or die trying."

"Do I need to call the cavalry?" Jonno asked after a pause. "A few of them are in the neighborhood, and the rest can be located fairly quickly."

Dex shook his head and looked over at Monty. "You're doing more than I can ask by taking us to the nexus. No, I don't want this rippling back on the Ten. LD and TK are going to take enough heat for this, but they have the boutique."

"They can disappear, I know." Jonno looked to the rear of the plane. LD was holding TK's hand, and she was resting her head back with her eyes closed. "We can make ourselves pretty scarce, but if they come after us with runic trackers, they'll find us eventually."

"This is why you're only taking us to the nexus. We'll make our own way back."

"What do you mean by going in dark?" I had a bad feeling about what he meant, but I wanted to make sure. "That means lights off?"

Jonno gave me a crooked smile. "The energy at the nexus will fry us if it senses any overt runic activity. We have dampeners to combat some of its defenses, but we don't take any chances. 'We go dark' means everything gets shut off, and we glide in with an assist at the end."

"He's kidding, right?" I looked at Dex, who wasn't smiling. "Is he serious? We're gliding in with an assist?"

"Now you know why TK hates flying with René."

TWENTY-ONE

JONNO RETURNED TO the cockpit after sharing our landing strategy and scaring the hell out of me. I felt like moving to the back with TK. I wondered if LD could surround me with a shock-absorbing orb in case our landing was by collision with the nexus.

"Over here, lad." Dex tapped me on the shoulder. "You need something to keep your brain active. Let's work on your orbs."

I gave him a look because this was Dex, and I never knew exactly what he meant.

"My what?"

He cupped his hands in front of him and looked at me as if that was supposed to make it clearer. "Your orbs. I hear they're shriveled up and useless."

"I don't think my orbs are any of your business, no offense." I leaned over and glanced at Monty, who was doing a great job at fake-sleeping, except for the small smile across his lips. "Was this Monty? He's never seen my orbs."

"It wasn't the pup." Dex looked down at Peaches.

"Let's have it, then, show me what you got."

I was about to unleash a set of extra colorful curses going back several generations, to my Hispanic maternal grandmother, when Monty interrupted.

"He means your Incantation of Light," Monty said without turning. I could hear the smile in his voice. "And they do need work, unless you plan on unleashing anemic raisins at accomplished mages who will blast you where you stand."

"They're getting better," I lied. "Now they're almost the size of apples."

"Perhaps upon seeing your desiccated Apples of Destructive Might, the Sanctuary mages will surrender to your greater magical ability." He turned to face me. "Show my uncle your almighty Incantation of Light orb."

"Well, of course I mean his Incantation of Light." Dex looked at Monty, confused. "What else would I mean?"

I held my hand out and focused.

"Igniscoruscanti," I whispered, forming an orb of violet energy. It was about the size of a grapefruit and hovered in my palm. I felt the energy race up my arm and suffuse my body with warmth.

I looked at Monty with a smug smile as he glanced down at my hand and pointed. I felt the orb begin to shrink. It kept shrinking until it was the size of a grape. I concentrated and imagined pumping energy into it. The next second, it popped like a soap bubble and disappeared.

Dex nodded for a few seconds, trying to keep a straight face. He burst into laughter after I stared at him.

"I'm sorry, lad," he said in-between guffaws. "That was the saddest orb I have ever seen. How did you make it pop like that at the end?"

"I think you may be suffering from premature orb formation," Monty said seriously as Dex held his breath. "Sometimes those orbs are hard to keep firm."

Dex burst into laughter again.

"Oh, you two are hilarious," I snapped back. "I see this incredible sense of humor is a genetic defect."

The laughter did help, actually. It was good to see Monty attempt a smile, even if it was at my expense. It helped keep the thoughts about his rapid aging in the back of my mind.

"Come here, lad." Dex waved me over. "I'll help you massage it into shape." He almost burst into another fit of laughter. "Sorry, I meant I'll give you a hand."

He let out another burst of laughter as I waited, staring at him. His face hit beet red, and he was short of breath by the time he composed himself.

"Are you done?"

He nodded and waved me over again. "Sit down over here." He patted the chair in front of him.

I sat across from him and swiveled the chair to face him.

"Who taught you this spell?"

"Thomas the traitor," I growled. "While we were in London."

"Ach, there's your problem right there." Dex pointed at me. "Every time you use this spell, you're angry. It'll never work that way. You have to let go of the anger and the hate."

"He tried to kill me, Monty, and Peaches," I shot back. "You want me to have warm, fuzzy thoughts about him?"

Peaches opened an eye, looked at me, and raised his head.

<Do you need me to lick you? My saliva also has calming properties.>

<I'm fine, no thanks.>

<Do you need meat? I always feel better after eating meat. Is there any meat around? Are you going to make some?>

<I'll get you some meat later. Why don't you go back to your nap?>

<I will. If you need a lick or make some meat, I'm right here.>

<Good to know, thanks.>

He closed his eyes and settled back down. A few seconds later, he was snoring.

Dex looked at me. "You have to let go of the hate and anger. Casting is all about being in control. You're not a mage, so you don't have the benefit of years of training. If you try and cast this way it will lead you to —"

"The dark side?"

"Are you daft? What dark side? It will lead you to sprain that thick skull of yours. The hate and anger get in the way of control. Are you going to take this seriously or not?"

"I'm sorry, I thought you were going to go all Yoda on me for a moment."

"Yogurt? Who's talking about curdled milk? We're talking magic here, boy."

"I was just making a reference to—"

He waved my words away and held up a finger, silencing me.

"Light, dark, and everything in between depends on the magic-user. The energy isn't good or bad. It all comes down to the wielder. Now...pay attention!"

He flicked me on the forehead with his index finger. I heard a chuckle from the rear of the plane and caught LD covering his face and looking to the side.

"Fine, show me what I need to do."

"The first thing we need to change is the word of power."

TWENTY-TWO

"ARE YOU SURE it's safe to do this in here?" I looked around the plane and especially in the direction of the cockpit.

"We can't very well go outside now, can we?"

"That's not what I meant. I mean what if I lose control and damage René's plane?"

"I strongly advise against that. She's quite particular about her plane."

"That's not helping. We're in a pressurized environment. If the orb punches a hole in the plane, we can crash—or worse, explode."

"Oh, that would make René extremely angry indeed."

"Dex, this is serious. We should do this someplace like the Danger Room at the boutique."

"Deadly serious, yes. Consider it incentive to get focused."

"Why am I even doing this?" I threw my hands up in the air, frustrated. "The Sanctuary will be locked down against magic. I won't even be able to use this spell."

"Let's say for a moment that you learn the spell, I

mean really learn it."

"Hard to believe, but okay. Then what? I'm still in a place where I don't have access to magic."

"Unless that access is changed somehow," he answered. "The mages will see you as a special human most likely, but not a threat. Except, you know a spell, you have a—"

"A magic missile," I finished. "They'll never expect that from me."

"Well, to be honest, I don't expect much from you either, but let's give it a go, shall we?"

"Well, I'm all confident now, thanks."

"You're welcome. Now, focus. Did he teach you the pattern to the incantation?"

I did the complicated pattern Thomas had taught me. It still felt like watching the third-base coach telling me to steal home before the next pitch. Dex nodded in approval as I went through the different gestures.

"That was bloody excellent."

"Thank you, it took a while before I got the entire pattern down and—"

"And bloody useless. Forget it, forget all of it."

"What? Thomas said it was necessary to learn the pattern."

"Bollocks." Dex leaned back in his chair, steepled his fingers, and stared at me. "Do you know why mages do all the finger-wiggling and gesturing?"

"Because the gestures unlock the mysteries of the cosmos?"

"Who sold you that load of shite? If that were the case, I'd be all enlightened by now, which I can guarantee you, I'm not."

"I thought the gestures were special diagrams symbolizing contained power and runes."

He leaned forward. "So what you're saying is, if I scratch my arse or pick my nose, I'm unlocking power? What power am I using now?"

He proceeded to extend his middle finger into my face.

"None."

"Damn right. All of that is rubbish. You train with that...Master Yak, don't you?"

"Master Yat." I nodded. "If you call practiced agony training, then yes."

"He teaches you drills, doesn't he? Forms that you have to learn to remember the techniques, yes?"

"Yes, he calls them kata or prearranged forms. It helps me remember groups of techniques by grouping them into a prearranged sequence."

"And when you face off against an enemy, do you fight with the kata?"

"No, that would get me killed. The techniques are modified to fit the situation."

He leaned back and stared at me. It took a moment, but it dawned on me. He nodded when the realization hit.

"Tell me," he said, glancing over at Monty. "Tell me why the gestures exist."

"They're kata?"

He slapped my knee and grinned before becoming serious again. "Most mages think the gestures are the key to using their magic. Those of us who are older are a bit wiser."

"The gestures are shorthand to the runes, but it's

deeper than that," I said, putting it together. "The study and years of training. The runes affect the energy around us, but it comes down to the will. This is why mages don't use a focus. They are the focus."

He pointed at me and nodded. "It comes down to manipulating energy and use of will. Even the words of power are just giving energy shape and form. Those are used when the spell has a unique component."

He held his hand in front of me, palm up. With his other hand, he pointed at his palm.

"A special component?"

"This incantation requires life force. In your case, since you've been cursed by Kali to have an abundance of this, it becomes an especially dangerous spell. Do you understand?"

"Being immortal means I have an unlimited supply of magic missiles?"

"We'll call that close enough." He shook his head and looked down at his hand. I followed his eyes as he spoke quietly. "*Ignisvitae.*"

A green orb of power the size of a basketball formed in the center of his palm and floated just above his hand. I felt the energy coming off the orb in waves. He looked at me, grinned, and closed his hand around the orb, absorbing it. He nodded to me.

"You want me to do that?"

"Use the word and create the orb. No gestures, no anger or hate. Just focus and make the orb."

"Dex, is that a good idea?" LD said from the back. "He won't be able to control it if he does make one."

Dex swiveled his chair to face LD.

"Have you seen his orbs?" he said with a chuckle.

"They're the size of grapes. Besides, it takes years to master an Incantation of Light. We're safe. This is just an exercise to get him to stretch his—"

"*Ignisvitae*," I whispered and felt a rush of power. It raced down my arm and pooled in my hand, coalescing.

"Uncle Dex," Monty said, staring at me, "you may want to reconsider…"

"Dex!" LD yelled and pointed at me. "Shit!"

I held a violet orb of power about two feet in diameter in the palm of my hand. The energy of the orb coursed through my arm.

Dex turned and stared at the orb in my hand, and then he stared in my eyes. "That's not a grape-sized orb, lad." He kept his voice calm and modulated, and I realized LD was right. I had no idea what to do with this orb.

"I don't think I can hold on to it, Dex. It wants to push off my hand. Should I focus more?"

"No! I mean no," he said quickly. "Bloody hell, you've surprised us all, but now we—and by we I mean you—need to get rid of that orb."

Holding on to the orb felt like trying to push the two like poles of magnets together. It wanted to push it off my hand and I had to keep adjusting to maintain its position.

"Do I just close my hand like you did?"

"Let's start with that." He nodded and I saw his hands give off a green glow. "I'll try to give you a hand."

Out of the corner of my eye, I saw Monty start gesturing.

Jonno's voice came over the intercom. "In an effort

to save time and fuel, we've bisected the Bermuda Triangle. We're approaching the point near Puerto Rico where we will experience the greatest runic turbulence."

"It doesn't surprise me that she went through the Triangle," TK said, raising her voice as her eyes began to glow a deeper green. "She's trying to kill us!"

"TK, trying to focus here, thank you," Dex said, never taking his eyes off the orb.

"Please fasten your seatbelts," Jonno's calm voice continued. "From there we will head south and hug the coast of Brazil. Please strap in, the Triangle is bumpy at the best of times. Once past, we will begin our approach to the nexus. Thank you."

"Oh, bugger," Dex said as the plane lurched up and then slammed down. The orb bounced out of my hand and shot down the aisle to the rear of the plane as we stared at its trajectory. "That's not good."

LD was already moving. He gestured and formed a lattice of gray energy in his fingers. The Strix shifted to the right and yawed, throwing us against the wall. LD missed the orb as the lattice sailed past me and enveloped Dex.

"Bollocks!" I saw Dex wrestling with the lattice as it wrapped itself around him and constricted his movement.

TK and Monty, the only two who were still wearing seatbelts, swiveled their chairs and cast a spell, which intercepted the orb with a black and golden lattice and suspended it mid-cabin. It remained frozen in place, and I breathed a sigh of relief as the orb vibrated against the forces holding it there.

"LD, try and siphon the energy from it, that way

Simon can absorb what's left," Dex said as he undid the lattice from around his body.

"On it." LD approached the orb unsteadily as the plane lurched and bounced. He gestured as he stepped close.

"Brilliant idea, Dex." TK glared at him. "Why don't we have the immortal use his life force to create an orb that can basically punch through *anything*, while we're in a plane?"

"Make it quick, boy," Dex hissed, ignoring TK. "We hit any more runic turbulence and it'll punch a hole right through the Strix."

I approached the orb from the other end and closed the distance, using the chairs to keep me from falling over as I headed down the aisle. LD did the same.

René's voice came over the intercom. "TK, are you secured safely in your seat?"

"Of course I'm secured in my seat, you maniac!" TK yelled back. "You should rename this piece of flying debris the Ostrich. You fly almost as well as one!"

"Just checking," René singsonged over the intercom. "Wouldn't want any of my passengers to experience discomfort as we evade the next wave of runic turbulence."

"What wave of runic turbulence?" TK asked.

"Please brace yourselves," René said over the intercom. "We will be leaving the Triangle and the worst of the turbulence shortly."

I heard Dex curse and secure his seatbelt. Monty gestured, forming a violet lattice that descended on Peaches and secured him in place.

"You wouldn't dare," TK hissed as black energy

covered her arms. "I'm going to strangle her."

LD and I both stared at each other. "Oh, shit," I said.

We moved to close in on the orb as the plane ascended and entered a canopy roll. LD and I bounced off the ceiling, into the lattice holding the orb, and landed in a heap. The Strix was still shaking from the turbulence when I heard the high-pitched whine.

The orb, reacting to the force we had applied to the lattice, shot straight up and out of the Strix, blasting a hole in the cabin.

"That wasn't me!" I looked up into the hole as klaxons blared and red emergency lights flashed throughout the plane.

"Strap in," LD said, pushing me to the front and then gesturing. "It's going to get dicey on the approach."

I ran to the chair opposite Dex and strapped in. Dex grinned at me and patted me on the knee. "I'd say that was a good first attempt."

I stared at him as the cockpit door slammed open behind me.

"What happened to my plane?" René screamed as she approached the extra ventilation my magic missile had provided. She whirled on TK, who was sitting, quietly wrapped in black energy, and staring back at her.

"It wasn't me, but if you like, I can finish the dismantling of this flying heap you call a plane."

"Do *not* insult the Strix." René pointed at TK and glared. "Be thankful we were flying so low, or we'd all be gasping for air in freefall right now."

"LD will take care of it." Dex grabbed René by the wrist. "Get us to the nexus."

"He'd better get it fixed, Dex," she growled and pulled her arm away before heading back to the front.

René stomped back into the cockpit, slamming the door behind her. A few seconds later, Jonno ran out and joined LD as they reformed the Strix.

"We're approaching the nexus," René's angry voice came over the intercom. "If you can manage to refrain from punching any more holes in the Strix, we will land in two minutes. We're going in dark, which means no magic use."

The klaxons turned off and the plane went dark. I could still see the faint gray glow surrounding LD and Jonno as they repaired the plane.

"That should do it." LD sat in a chair and gasped. "I need a vacation."

Jonno looked at the location where the magic missile had broken through the cabin. He placed his hand on it and the ceiling was covered in a light blue glow. After a few seconds, he nodded and the glow subsided.

"Nice work, LD," Jonno muttered as he examined the repair again. "I'll have to take her to the shop for a thorough fix but it should hold for now."

"You won't be able to stay on the nexus long." LD nodded and rested his head back. "Drop us and get the hell away."

Jonno bumped fists with LD and glanced back at the green glow that was surrounding TK, before heading over to Dex. "This smells just like you, Dex. No more magic practice until you are off the Strix."

Dex held his hands up in mock surrender. "I don't know what you're talking about."

"No more magic, I'm serious."

"Jonno," René's voice came over the intercom, "T-minus one twenty."

Jonno headed back to the cockpit and shot Dex one more look before closing the door.

"It's almost like they don't trust me." Dex looked over to where TK sat, still glowing green and simmering.

"Yeah, I wonder why that is?" Peaches, now free from the lattice, came over and plopped at my feet. The runes on his collar pulsed in the low light conditions, as did my matching bracelet.

<*The angry man isn't feeling well.*>

<*I know, boy. But he'll get better soon.*>

<*If I lick him, he will get better.*>

<*Let's save the saliva therapy for later. Right now, he needs to rest. We have a lot of work to do.*>

I ran my hand over Peaches' collar and felt the energy pulse along its length. "Dex, why do we have to go in dark, again?"

"The nexus is covered with a dense runic field that acts as a defensive measure. Any runic activity on approach activates it. Once we're on the island, we can cast, but even that is dangerous. I wouldn't cast more than a teleportation circle on the nexus. Why?"

"The limiter and my bracelet." I held up my wrist holding the pulsing stones. "Do these count as runic ability?"

"Ten seconds to touchdown," René said over the intercom.

The air in the cabin shifted, and I felt the hair on the back of my arms stand on end as it became charged. I saw small arcs of red energy dance between Peaches and me.

Fear filled Dex's eyes as he realized my observation. The fear I saw in his eyes kick-started the voice in my head into full-blown panic. I slapped the voice upside the head and grabbed it by the throat until it shut up.

Dex flung green discs of energy at all of us. He shoved Peaches and me away and tossed the last two discs through the cockpit door, as a bolt of bright red energy sliced through the Strix where I had been standing seconds earlier, severing the cabin in half. We fell for half a second before a green flash blinded me.

TWENTY-THREE

PARTS OF THE Strix littered the island we stood on. Above us, the sky was a borealis on steroids as the runic defenses danced across it in a kaleidoscope of color. I looked around to take in where we were. The nexus was about half a square mile of flat, featureless land.

There were no structures or buildings of any type. The only indication that someone had been here before us were the large circles covered in runes off to one side from where we arrived. Nothing grew on the island. I figured the lack of vegetation was due to the excess magic.

LD and TK were doing something near the circles. Dex was out of earshot, speaking to a screaming René. Jonno stood next to her, looking about as displeased as she sounded. Monty, looking more like his regular, scowly self, stood next to me and took in the lack of scenery.

"I think your destructiveness is contagious." I looked around at the debris that used to be the Strix. "Maybe it's a virus? Like a tristanullificationterminus virus. It causes the infected to obliterate things in proximity against their will."

"A virus?"

"I could call it MontyNT? Guaranteed to leave an impression, or is that 'depression'?"

He stared at me and then looked off into the distance before answering. "Your brain is very similar to the nexus, Simon."

"Colorful and mysterious." I nodded solemnly. "I get that a lot."

He turned to face me. "I was thinking more along the lines of 'empty and devoid of substance.'"

"Well, it's good to see old age hasn't affected that cutting wit of yours," I grumbled. "Sharp as a butter knife."

"Didn't our brief visit to London teach you anything about listening to my uncle?" He looked over to where Dex and René were still conversing.

It was actually more Dex standing there as René waved her arms and yelled at him. Every so often, I could hear Dex's baritone voice interject, and René would launch into another tirade.

"Are you saying the Strix was my fault?" I held up the pulsing entropy bracelet. "If I remember correctly, this whole limiter idea was yours to begin with."

"It wasn't entirely your fault. The limiter should have been masked or dampened." He scowled and for a moment looked like his normal self. "If I weren't preoccupied with other matters, like my accelerated aging, I would have addressed that. My apologies."

"At least you look better." I glanced over at him. "Is that because you used a reservoir?"

He nodded. "I need to be judicious about their use." He looked down at his fingers. The black bands glistened in the morning sun. They were simple rings with intricate runes etched into the surface. One of them had faded to a lighter color, appearing more gray than black.

"How long does each reservoir last?"

"Depends on what spells I cast, it seems." He held up the finger with the gray ring. "The lattices I used to contain your orb and creature were costly because they're designed to remain constant, drawing power from me—or from the reservoirs, in this case."

"And one of your flame orbs of obliteration?"

"Should be a minimal expenditure of energy, depending on the size of the target."

"So orb-flinging and blowing up buildings, yes. Force fields and prolonged spells, no."

"This from the person who just destroyed a state-of-the-art, one-of-a-kind stealth plane with…what do you call it? A magic missile?"

"That wasn't my fault. Dex suggested we try it on the plane, of all places." I held up the bracelet again. "Besides, it wasn't the missile that destroyed the Strix. It was Peaches' limiter and this crazy bracelet."

"True, he should've known better, but he's Dex. He also managed to get us off the plane safely. Sometimes I think he does it deliberately."

"I didn't know you could throw teleportation circles like that."

"I can't." He shook his head and almost smiled. "I doubt there are any mages on the planet, besides my uncle, who can execute a multiple teleport mid-flight as the plane is disintegrating around us. Uncle Dex is a prodigy in many of the things he manages to do, including angering people."

"René sounds pissed." I looked over to where she stood. "Not that I blame her. The Strix was a nice plane."

A green flash caught my eye and René and Jonno were gone. Dex came over to where we stood and narrowed his eyes at Monty.

"She didn't want to say goodbye?" I looked over to where the green glow faded.

"Actually she did, but it required inflicting each of us with incredible amounts of pain." He shook his head. "I promised to get her another Strix, and she calmed down to only wanting to maim us."

"Were you trying to get us killed?" Monty asked. "You know Simon isn't a mage and has no training."

"Perfect—no bad habits to unlearn." He narrowed his eyes at Monty again. "How much did you use?"

"I'm fine." Monty waved away the words. "Cecil won't be able to get her a Strix, you know."

"I know. I have a contact in Division 13. They'll get her a new one. They owe the Ten."

"*You* have a contact in Division 13?" Monty raised an eyebrow. "Why am I not surprised."

"I do." It was Dex's turn to wave the words away. "They'll get her a new Strix with all the latest gadgets. She may not be giving us any rides in the near future. At least, not until she calms down."

"She's always been attached to her planes," LD said as he walked over. "How's Jonno?"

"A lot calmer than René. Out of the two, he's the

more dangerous."

"I still remember his wind tunnel." LD shuddered. "You don't want him pissed at you."

"Did you prep our arrival?" Dex looked down at the circles. "We have to get in without tripping the outer defenses."

"I can breach the outer defenses and the wall." He glanced at TK, whose eyes were no longer glowing green. "After the breach, we'll maintain the exit. Once inside, you'll have to do the heavy lifting."

"Can you compensate for the limiter?" Dex pointed at my wrist. "We all dropped the ball on that one."

"That was sloppy. I didn't think it would set off the nexus. Apparently, it's not as dormant as I thought it would be."

"Is this going to be a problem?" Dex frowned, looking down at Peaches' collar.

"Maybe the hellhound can wait outside with TK and me?" LD suggested.

Dex cocked his head to one side. "You haven't dealt with hellhounds much, have you?"

"I know they like to eat and destroy. He's actually perfect for this group."

TK stepped forward and rubbed Peaches' ears. "You can't hold a hellhound. His bond allows him to follow Simon anywhere. He's better off going with them. We can hold the breach." She turned to LD. "You can use the inverted masking rune on the limiter, darling. It should do the job in the short term."

LD nodded. "That could work. Give me a few minutes." He stepped to one of the circles and began drawing symbols into the existing design.

"How long can you hold it open before you need to abandon the breach?" Monty asked, looking over to where LD was working.

"LD will be keeping it open, that's his strength." TK looked down at her hands. "Mine is making sure he stays alive. You have three days at most before he's too weak to maintain the exit. Then we leave, with or without you."

"Excuse me? Three days?" LD grinned as he looked up from the circle. "You underestimate my greatness, dear. This is not my first break-in."

"It's the first time you've infiltrated the Sanctuary." She gave him the 'if you continue down this road, only pain awaits you' smile. "It would be better to be conservative and not dead. Don't you think, *darling*?"

"How many?" Dex crouched down and examined the circle with the inverted masking rune. "And don't stretch it. I'll not be answering to TK for your demise."

"I can give you four, max. This is not my first break-in," LD said again, oblivious to TK's smile of impending doom. "If we get caught, it may be my last, though."

"You're opening the door," Dex said, his tone serious. "We're the ones going in. Your job is to make sure we can get out once we're done. Or to make sure no one gets out if we fail. Three days. If we're not at the exit by then, you're gone."

TK nodded but remained silent.

LD brushed off his hands and stood. "We're ready. You want to check the circles before I start?"

Dex looked them over and crouched down, pointing to one side. He and LD discussed something in hushed tones. TK gestured and materialized a sausage for Peaches.

<*She's still scary, but I like her. She makes the best meat.*>

<*I'll let her know.*>

<*Please do. Let her teach you how to make the magic meat.*>

<*I'll inform her that she has passed your seal of approval.*>

"Peaches says thank you, and that your choice of meat happens to be his favorite."

TK smiled and rubbed Peaches' ears again.

"He is most welcome."

"Your opinion on this, nephew." Dex called out and Monty headed over to where LD and Dex were crouched.

"What is Division 13?" I asked, looking at TK as she kept rubbing Peaches. "How are they going to produce a plane that runs about sixty-five million without the bells and whistles?"

"Dex isn't part of the Ten." She stood and moved away from the circles. "He's been invited several times, but he's just too free a spirit."

"I get that from him," I said. "He doesn't like being tied down."

"The same thing happened at the Sanctuary. He could have easily been an Elder by now, but he chose his freedom over the constraints of leadership."

"What does this have to do with this Division 13? How is he connected to it?"

"I don't know the details," she answered. "But I'll tell you what he told me when I asked about them."

"What did he say?"

"He told me he needed to help them," she replied quietly. "He said, 'He who fights with monsters should see to it that he himself doesn't become a monster.'"

"Was he talking about them or himself?"

"I don't know. Maybe one day you can ask him."

TWENTY-FOUR

WE WALKED OVER and joined Dex, LD and Monty.

"This isn't a teleportation." LD pointed at the circle beneath us. "It's nothing as delicate or finessed as that."

"Then what is it?" I feared for my digestive system. "And how much will I throw up when we arrive?"

LD chuckled. "You should be fine, more or less. What we're going to do is more of a temporal shove."

TK nodded. "That was actually an apt description, darling."

"Thank you, dear. I thought you'd like it."

"I do." She waved a hand. "Carry on."

"In order for all of us to make the trip, you need to be in sync with me. This is a Sanctuary failsafe so no one accidentally finds it."

"So you can't just Croft your way into the Sanctuary?"

"Correct. I don't have an issue with the hellhound. I think he can pretty much go wherever he wants, but you aren't a mage, so we need to get your thoughts aligned."

"How do we do that?"

"For this trip, you need to think like a mage."

"You mean, I need to be deranged and think in concepts that make no sense, even though I'm using English to describe them?"

LD glanced up from the runes he was working on in the circle. "He sounds like you, Dex."

"Mages occasionally get caught in their echo chambers, yes. This is why we probably prefer to be alone." TK gestured and materialized a spoon in her hand. "What am I showing you right now, Simon? What do you see?"

Somehow, I knew this was a trick question. I narrowed my eyes in my best Eastwood squint, easily a three on my glare-o-meter, and gave her the answer I thought she wanted to hear.

"That… there is no spoon."

I was confident I had koaned the hell out of her question, and smiled smugly.

She looked at me, looked at the spoon, and then looked at me again. She held the spoon up a little higher. My eyes tracked it as she slid the spoon side to side and then thwacked me in the center of the forehead.

"Does that feel like I'm not holding a spoon?"

"Ow! What the hell?"

LD and Dex chuckled, and Monty turned away with a smile almost crossing his lips. The pain radiated outward from the center of my forehead. I rubbed it as she stared at me. Peaches chuffed at my feet.

<I can bite her, but she might do something nasty and painful to you. Also, she may not make any more meat for me. That

would not be good.>

<So glad your first concern is not for my safety but for your supply of sausage.>

<You told me to focus on the important things. She makes the best meat. Meat is life.>

<I thought a bondmate was supposed to be the most important thing to a hellhound?>

<Right after meat, you are the most important thing.>

<Good to know where I stand.>

<On your feet, like always? Did she hit your head too hard?>

TK sighed and looked at LD. "Maybe we can leave him and the hellhound here?"

"No," Monty said quietly. "Show him. Use a transference burst."

TK looked at Dex, who nodded. "We need to get off the nexus, and we're running out of time. It's the fastest way."

"He's not a mage," she answered. "The pain…"

"No choice." Dex put a hand on my shoulder. "Don't take this personally, but your brain just doesn't function like a mage. This is to help you see things differently enough to get you to the Sanctuary. It's going to hurt."

"What kind of pain are we talking here? Is it like a migraine or something? Do I get a warning or will—?"

TK placed two fingers on my forehead and images blasted into my brain. The pain was a migraine, followed by the feeling of an axe splitting my skull open.

This allowed the jackhammer to pound my brain to a mushy pulp so it could drain out my ears. This was then followed by an ample dose of hydrochloric acid to clean out what was left.

Finally, she used a blowtorch to distract me from the pain and seared everything to dust as I nearly collapsed, holding my head. LD and Dex held me up when my legs stopped working. I heard Peaches whine at my feet. She removed her fingers from my forehead and the pain subsided.

"Monitor the hellhound," I heard her say from a distance. "He's going to experience some backlash along their bond."

I thought she was done, when she placed two fingers on my forehead again. She said something under her breath and the Vulcan mind-meld from hell started again with the migraine. The cycle repeated, and I started to scream. I blacked out shortly after that.

TWENTY-FIVE

I OPENED MY eyes to a rainbow sky.

TK stepped into my field of vision. She flashed a light in my eyes and nodded. "He's back."

"Good, we need to get off this rock," Dex growled. "I'm starting to feel the effects of the runic interference."

She held up the spoon in front of my face. I felt the warm flush of my curse deal with whatever damage I had just gone through. All I wanted to do was lie down and sleep for a few centuries, except it hurt to breathe and think.

"What did you do?" I was groggy and sore all at once.

"Simon," she said in a low voice, "what do you see?"

"A spoon," I answered, upset. "What did you expect me to see? You melted my brain just so I could explain to you that you're holding a simultaneously convex and concave construct designed to displace food?"

"He's ready," she said with a smile. "I don't know how long it will last, so let's go, darling."

"Watching you work is just...wow, dear."

"Eloquent as always, darling. Can we go now?"

LD shifted to the circle under us as I looked on in wonder. I actually understood what he was doing. The symbols he manipulated were clear. I understood their purpose and how they interacted with each other. I bent down to touch one of the symbols, and Dex smacked my hand, standing me up.

"I can see it, Dex," I said in awe. "I understand it now. I can help. It's only a matter of shifting the temporal axis several degrees until we align with the Sanctuary's position in time and space."

"Not bad," LD said from the ground as he manipulated more of the symbols. "Keep the newly enlightened member of the team away from the symbols so we're not scattered all over the place."

TK grabbed my arm and gently but firmly guided me away from LD.

"What did you do to me and why do I sound like Monty?"

"I gave your brain a little nudge and accelerated your understanding a bit. It's just firing a bit faster now."

"You used your creative ability to augment the synaptic firing rate and load capacity of my neurons?" The words spilled out, and I looked at her, surprised. "How did I do that?"

"How long will it last?" Dex asked. "More importantly, did you give him brain damage?"

"Not very long." TK raised her voice and glanced at LD.

"Don't rush me, woman," LD muttered under his breath. "This isn't as easy as I make it look."

"I can't give him another transference." TK looked at me and pulled me back as I started drifting over to where LD was working on the runes. "I'm surprised he survived this one. He should be a basket case or comatose after that."

"I would attribute it to the protective measures of the curse that is currently keeping my body in a state of molecular stasis. This prevents my body from aging or taking damage," I said. "If you allow me to assist LD, I'm certain I can expedite the process and remove us from this location, before any of you suffer from the detrimental effects of exposure."

"Wonderful," Dex said with a sigh. "That sounds like a great idea, but why don't we let LD get us to the Sanctuary?"

"I was merely offering an alternative to the less-than-efficient approach LD is utilizing. Aren't we on a limited timetable?"

LD looked up and shot me a look. "Excuse me? Less than efficient?"

I nodded as Dex dragged me over to the other side of the circle. "There are three—no, four—other ways you can arrange those runes to create a quantum bridge and transport us to the Sanctuary. All of them faster than the method you are currently employing. Would you like me to demonstrate them to you?"

"I'm not feeling this suddenly magey Simon," LD snapped. "Keep him over there until I'm done."

"He does have a point, darling," TK said gently. "We're running out of time."

LD threw his hands up. "Do you want to have Mage Einstein over there transport us to the Sanctuary?"

"No, of course not. I was merely stating that we are short on time."

"If I weren't being interrupted every five seconds…"—he refocused on the runes in front of him— "I'd be done by now."

I looked down at Peaches, who looked up at me and cocked his head to one side.

<Are you still attuned to the frequency of my thoughts, bondmate?>

I nodded. *<Apparently so, although you do sound different.>*

<It would seem that whatever process the mage put your brain through is allowing you to modulate your brain waves to my higher frequency.>

<Are you implying this is your normal pattern of thought?>

<Affirmative. However, when I attempted to communicate with you, I found it to be impossible and thus needed to shift my brainwaves to a more primitive level.>

<I understand. I'm not particularly known for dwelling in the realm of higher thought. This is quite a surprise even for me.>

<That would explain their distrust of your offers of help. Although your methodology may be sound, their prior experience of you doesn't align with your successful manipulation of runic symbols to facilitate a bridge.>

<Point taken.>

<I could really use some protein. A hellhound body burns a tremendous amount of energy, which means I need to keep myself regularly supplied with meat as a source of fuel.>

<You know, there is a high probability I can make some meat for you. I have seen most of them use the gestures. It's not overly difficult.>

<I refer back to my earlier statement of your not handling

runic energy with any kind of expertise. The destruction of the flying vessel was in part due to your use of magic.>

<Yes, but my thought processes have been accelerated, providing me with knowledge I did not possess heretofore.>

<If it means the creation of sustenance with meat products, then I am in accord. Let us commence. I eagerly await your creation of protein.>

Everyone else was focused on LD and his forming of the bridge to get us to the Sanctuary. I turned my back, practiced the gestures I had seen TK execute, and nodded once to Peaches.

<The pattern is firmly in mind. This either creates the most delicious sausage in the history of sausage or opens a direct portal to the Sanctuary. I'm not certain.>

<How can you not be certain? Those are two very distinct objectives.>

<Honestly, I think my mage brain is reverting to normal brain function.>

<As much as I enjoy and appreciate meat, for meat is life, I must advise against this course of action. It jeopardizes us all.>

<I can do this. Meat sausage for the win!>

I gestured and poured my will into creating the best sausage for Peaches. After several tries, nothing happened.

A muffled explosion went off behind me, and I turned in time to see LD launched out of the circle and across the ground for several feet.

"What the hell?" he yelled as he started walking back to the circle. "Which one of you cast while I'm performing a delicate runic construction so we can enter the Sanctuary *without* being noticed?"

They all turned to face me.

<This is very bad.>

<I agree. I thought for sure I had your sausage. Well, at least I didn't create a doorway to the Sanctuary. That would've been really bad.>

A whoosh and the sound of metal across stone cut through the silence behind LD.

"Were you trying to pay us a visit?" a voice said as a rift opened. "It's considered the height of poor manners to invade a home without an invitation. And I don't recall seeing your invitation."

A figure stepped through the rift, dressed in a black suit with a golden circle on the lapel. His thin frame gave off waves of energy as he leaned forward on his walking stick.

LD turned around and backed up. "Oh, shit. Is that Wenk?"

The man stood just outside the circle. His dark eyes glistened with deep violet power as he took in everyone. A slight smile played across his lips. He was tall, with salt-and-pepper hair cut short to his head. A long scar running down the left side of his face marred his otherwise flawless visage.

"I would be remiss if I didn't greet you properly, seeing as how you went through all this trouble. The Tushes, and not one, but two Montagues, accompanied by...who are you?"

"Strong. I'm—"

"You don't look particularly strong, but you do have a hellhound. Maybe I'll kill you last."

"That won't be necessary, Wenk." Dex stepped forward as green energy enveloped him.

"Oh no," Wenk said, his voice hardening as he stared

at Dex, "I insist. Would you believe I haven't even signaled the alarm? I wanted to see who would be so bold as to attempt a breach on the Golden Circle, in the Sanctuary no less."

"Oliver has you watching the perimeter now?" Dex stepped out of the circle. "What did he promise you?"

"What is rightfully ours," he said, reminding me of Gideon's last words. "I'm not just watching the perimeter. I guard the Sanctuary."

Dex narrowed his eyes and scowled. "He made you a Guardian? Where's Fen?"

"Fen retired, permanently. Afterwards, I became *the* Guardian." Wenk traced a finger down the scar on his face. "I never did properly thank you for this."

"I promise not to be so gentle this time," Dex replied, his voice hard and angry. "This time I'll finish the job."

Dex moved back, and I saw TK and LD flank him. They were moving into a tribus position like the one I saw at the boutique. Monty stepped to my side to protect the rear. I drew Grim Whisper and opened my jacket to give me access to Ebonsoul.

"How dangerous is this guy?" I asked Monty as he adjusted the reservoirs on his fingers. "Can Dex take him?"

"A Guardian is tasked with keeping the Sanctuary safe from any type of invasion—conventional or magical."

"This is the job of one person?"

Monty shook his hands out and stretched his neck. "One incredibly gifted person, yes."

"No kidding, he's a one-man army."

"After the Elders, he is the most powerful mage in the Sanctuary. He's also been given that siphon,"— Monty pointed at the walking stick— "which allows him to draw on the power of the Sanctuary."

"But we aren't in the Sanctuary."

"As long as that rift is open, he can access its power."

"What about the runic interference from the nexus?"

"He just got here. We've been here too long. He doesn't know that now, but he will, once our casting goes awry."

"How do we stop him?"

"If I can close the rift, you can use your magic missile."

"Hold on, the runic interference must be affecting my hearing, because I thought you said I could use my magic missile."

"Do you recall the conversation you had with my uncle on the Strix?"

"The one that helped blow a giant hole in the cabin?"

"Yes." He waved my words away, keeping his voice low. "Remember what he said about not expecting a magical attack from you?"

"Yes, my magic missile uses life force. So what?"

"It means you and your creature are the only ones here not affected by runic interference." Monty looked at the tribus formed by the others. "They don't have much longer."

I looked at them and realized their energy signatures were actually diminishing. If I could sense it, then so could Wenk.

"How long have you been on the nexus, Dex?" Wenk asked with a smile. "Your tribus is looking a bit peaked."

"It hasn't been long enough to stop us from handling a novice like you," Dex said as the green energy tightened around his body.

"You always were a horrible liar," Wenk said, shaking his head. "I guess I can bury all of you here. I promise to make it a burial befitting traitors and rogues."

"You two need to get clear, I'll handle this." Dex stepped forward and spread his arms.

TK shook out her arms as black energy arced all over her body. "We all go or we all stay. You know the code, Dex."

"No way, old man," LD said, gesturing. "Either we all go, or we all stay. Live or die."

"Today, it's die," Wenk said and slammed his stick into the ground.

TWENTY-SIX

LARGE CHUNKS OF earth floated into the air as the wave of dark orange energy from Wenk's strike raced across the ground. The tribus leaped into the air, avoiding the wave.

Dex landed on his feet, as did TK. LD landed and stumbled back, falling to one knee. Monty gestured and remained rooted. Peaches spread his forelegs, and the wave washed over him with no effect.

Unprepared, it bounced me about five feet out of the circle. I rolled into a crouch, took aim with Grim Whisper, and fired.

Wenk moved the walking stick and formed a wall in front of him, deflecting my bullets. A slab about three feet across hit me from the side and sent me sailing. I rolled and bounced for a few feet before coming to a stop.

<I'm going to bite him.>

<Please do. Give him an extra chomp from me.>

Peaches blinked out, reappeared next to Wenk, and looked ready to chomp on his leg, when a stone the size of a bowling ball slammed into his side and sent him sprawling. He shook it off and found his paws sinking into the ground.

<*Get out of there!*>

<*I'm stuck. The ground isn't normal.*>

Peaches kept sinking until only his head was visible. I noticed the ground he stood in gave off the same dark orange glow as the initial strike.

"Good boy. Stay," Wenk said, turning to face the others.

Monty raced around the perimeter of the circle as the tribus stepped to the center. They gestured in sync, simultaneously drawing and channeling energy. A swarm of black orbs, tinged with green and overlaid with gray, raced at Wenk.

Wenk stepped back to the rift and drove the stick into the ground. Monty started gesturing as he closed on Wenk. He shot me a look, our own form of shorthand, and I knew what he wanted.

The orbs closed on Wenk as he gestured. A wall of orange energy materialized in front of him. Monty unleashed a violet orb as the barrage crashed into the wall. Wenk lifted his stick and deflected Monty's orb, which shattered into a shower of riftrunes. A golden lattice formed over the rift, blocking it.

Wenk looked at the lattice, confused, as I whispered, "*Ignisvitae.*" The violet orb that formed in my palm was smaller this time, only about a foot across, but the energy it contained was overwhelming. I still didn't know how I was doing it. I only knew that I had to send it to Wenk, now. I extended my arm and pushed the orb at him. It blasted forward faster than I could track, punching a hole through the dark orange wall and through Wenk. He collapsed onto the ground a second later.

"The rift, now!" Dex yelled as we raced to the rapidly closing golden lattice. Dex gestured, lifting Wenk as TK dislodged Peaches, and we stepped through the rift.

TWENTY-SEVEN

"THE SANCTUARY IS in Cambodia?" I looked around and saw we were standing outside the wall of what looked like Ankgor Wat.

"No, Angkor Wat is the 'Sanctuary lite.' TK, I'm going to start the prep," LD said, moving to the nearest wall and gesturing rapidly. TK rushed to his side and gestured in sequence with him, but slower. "Angkor Wat was copied from the Sanctuary, not the other way around. One of the Elders was a strong influence on the Khmer Empire."

"How are you using magic? Monty said this would be a dead zone."

"It is. I'm not using runic energy. I'm doing this the same way you create your orb. Oh, and whatever you do…avoid the moat, if you like breathing."

"And this really isn't Cambodia?" I looked around in wonder at the similarities to the Ankgor Wat I knew. "It's almost identical."

"Not even close. The Sanctuary is an interstitial nexus point that makes the Moving Market look like a grocery store." He glanced quickly at TK. "No offense, hun."

"As long as you don't compare them to our boutique, none taken."

"Dex, he was telling the truth. No alarms. I'm starting the breach." LD rolled out a bag that held a set of rune-covered tools. "Breach in ten."

Wenk coughed up blood as Dex propped him up against the rough stone wall. The hole in his chest was much smaller than the orb I'd flung at him. He looked down at the wound and shook his head.

"The non-mage with an Incantation of Light. Clever," he said with a lopsided grin. "I guess the nexus drained all of us. Any other place, I would have stopped that orb."

"He surprised us, too." Dex examined the wound and shook his head slowly. "You don't have long, lad. Earth or fire?"

"Fire. Make sure I'm truly gone. I didn't expect it to be you," Wenk rasped as he looked up at Dex, "but I'm glad it was. You need to leave while you still can, Dex. Take them and don't turn back. Oliver is growing stronger every day. You won't be able to stop him."

Monty, holding Wenk's walking stick, gestured and closed the rift as white runes floated into the air.

"What is Oliver up to?" Dex looked at Wenk. "Why is he holding Connor?"

"Connor was the only threat from the Elders. He either turned or erased the others. But, he had nothing on Connor until he found her."

"Her?" Monty turned suddenly. "What do you mean, her?"

Wenk looked over at Monty and then back to Dex. "He's going to infiltrate the sects and take them from the inside. Use their power to usher in a new age of magic."

"Bloody hell," Dex said under his breath. "How? How is he planning this? He'll kill us all."

"Gray mages." Wenk coughed up more blood and gripped Dex's hand, looking at Monty. "You have to get him out of here. If Oliver gets him, he's won."

Monty stepped close, his face pale as beads of sweat covered his brow. "Wenk, who did he find? Who did he find to control Father?"

Wenk turned to face Monty and was about to speak, as another wave of coughs gripped his body. He caught his breath and gripped Monty by the shirt.

"Get out, Tristan. Now, while you still can. If he gets your essence, it's all over."

"Who? Who did he find?"

He stared into Monty's eyes. "He found your mother. He found Sara Montague."

"Impossible." Monty stumbled back from Wenk's words as if struck. "Lies. She's dead. Lies!"

Wenk looked back, his lifeless gaze and mute response unable to reply to Monty's accusation.

Dex grabbed Monty by the shoulder, hard. "Get a grip, lad! There's no way your mum's alive." Dex shook him once. "Whatever Oliver is using to control Connor is not your mother. Do you understand?"

"There's no way she can be alive," Monty repeated. "It must be an illusion of some kind."

"Exactly." Dex nodded. "It's a deception."

"My father is one of the strongest Elders in the

Golden Circle," Monty said under his breath. "How can Oliver deceive him?"

"Your father loved your mother with all he had. When she passed, I thought we would lose him, too." Dex looked at the wall of the Sanctuary. "If Oliver managed to convince Connor she was still alive, he wouldn't need to do much. Your father would prefer the illusion over a life without her."

"We're in," LD said, stepping back from the wall and wiping his forehead with his sleeve. "Before we activate this, I need to eat. I'm exhausted, and this is going take an insane amount of energy."

"How long?" Dex gestured, and sausages with bread appeared before all of us. Monty ignored his food and gave his sausage to Peaches, who promptly inhaled it. "How long can you hold the illusion and maintain the exit?"

"I know I said three days, but that was before we got Wenked," LD answered around a mouthful of sausage. "We stayed too long on the nexus, and I'm drained. Most I can give you is two days, and that's me pushing it with TK's help. After that, I'm fried and heading to a beach someplace warm to recover."

"Alone?" TK asked, raising an eyebrow. "Which beach?"

"I meant 'we,' dear," LD added quickly. "*We* are heading to a beach someplace warm."

"Just checking," she said with her scary smile. "It was truly going to be warm if you were going alone— hellish, even."

"I would never go on a vacation without you, dear." LD grinned. "I prefer to eat the barbecue, not be the barbecue."

She looked at Monty. "You need to eat. That stick can help only so much. If you siphon too much of the Sanctuary's energy, it could kill you."

Monty stared at her. She gestured and materialized another sausage with bread and a plate. "Some of us are more civilized than others." She glanced over at Dex, who shrugged. "Tristan, if you choose to perish from malnutrition, I will be forced to use the enforcement hammer on you. It will not be pleasant... for you."

"Who needs plates?" Dex said and continued devouring his sausage.

Monty took the plate, and Peaches looked up expectantly, hoping for another serving.

"I didn't know you cared," Monty answered as he looked at the sausage briefly before allowing Peaches to liberate it from his fingers.

"You and I *will* have our reckoning." Her voice was a jagged blade cutting through the air. "You will not die before that occurs. Or does the wordbond of a Montague no longer hold true?"

Both Monty and Dex stiffened at her words.

"We *will* have our reckoning," Monty said after a pause. "You have my word."

I shuffled back a bit, just in case they wanted to start the reckoning right at that moment.

"I know. Now, finish your food."

<Are you going to eat your meat?>

<Yes, I'm going to eat my meat. Hey, you don't sound smart anymore.>

<Guess what? Neither do you.>

Dex stepped close and inscribed runes on Wenk's body. He muttered something under his breath, and green flames engulfed Wenk. After a few seconds, nothing remained.

LD traced a diagram on the floor—a rough map of the Sanctuary.

"If I'm right, we are on the South Gallery and East Wing." He pointed to the lower right-hand corner of his map. "This place is called Heaven and Hells."

"The name is apt." Monty looked at the wall in front of us.

"What if you're wrong?" I looked down at his diagram.

"When it comes to maps, I'm never wrong, ever." LD shook his head. "My eidetic memory is flawless, and I have studied the plans of the Sanctuary more than once."

Dex nodded. "His brain records everything after seeing it just a single time. It has saved our lives more than once. His casting? Not so much."

LD glared at Dex with a smile, pointed, and continued.

"This is your exit point. You will not, I repeat, you will not be able to leave the Sanctuary any other way. Once you are through this point, the runic neutralizer comes into play."

"Do you have the ice?" Dex held out his hand. A subtle green glow covered his palm. "I'll take it now."

"Are you sure you want to use it?" LD glanced over at Monty. "Once you release it, there's no going back. We won't be there to save anyone who inhales that hell."

LD hesitated for a second and gestured. The black orb that appeared was surrounded by several gray orbs, each larger than the last, containing the mist in a Russian nesting doll of orbs.

"I'm sure." Dex extended his hand as the orb floated over to rest in the center of his palm. "This is called a last-resort weapon."

Dex closed his hand around the orb, and it disappeared.

"I thought you were the last-resort weapon?" LD stepped close to the wall, tapping sections of it. "Ready?"

Dex and Monty nodded at the same time. LD placed his hand on the wall, causing it to shimmer before it returned to its solid state.

"It didn't work?" I stepped up to the wall and pushed on the stone that was no longer there. LD grabbed me by the arm before I fell through the nonexistent wall.

"*Coño, hombre,*" LD hissed as he pulled me back. "Do you always think with your feet?"

"At least that time he was thinking," Monty said and slipped into the illusion of the wall.

"Forty-eight hours." Dex grabbed LD by the shoulder. "If we're not back by then, you bugger off."

LD nodded, and Dex stepped through the wall. I had recovered from my near fall, and TK approached.

"Every time he uses that stick, he will give away your position. If he relies too heavily on it, it will kill him. If that happens, I will hold you personally responsible."

She made several gestures, touching Peaches' collar and my bracelet.

"What was that?"

"Something to help you stay hidden from magical tracking. It won't work if they actually see you."

"You realize Monty is just another word for reckless, wanton destruction," I complained. "Now, I'm supposed to keep him alive?"

"Are you his friend?"

"Yes."

"Are you his family?"

"Absolutely."

"That is what family does. Use what Nana gave you and be his shieldbearer." She straightened out my jacket and brushed off some of the dirt. She stepped back a few feet, giving me a nod of approval. LD gave me a thumbs-up before refocusing on the wall. "Now, off with you."

"Have fun storming the Sanctuary," LD said, maintaining his focus on the wall as I stepped through with Peaches close to me.

TWENTY-EIGHT

I FOUND MYSELF in a dimly lit corridor. Peaches nudged my leg, nearly bouncing me into a wall as we started walking.

<Stop bumping into me.>

<It's not my fault you walk funny.>

<I what? You're the one who thinks he's larger than he really is.>

<I'm bigger on the inside. What's your excuse?>

<I—just because I don't grow to the size of a bus doesn't mean it's okay for you to bounce me off walls with your crazy walking.>

<Like I said, I'm bigger on the inside. And my walk isn't crazy. Dex said I saunter. I like that word, saunter.>

<Really? You're taking walking tips from Dex?>

<Saunter sounds like sausage. Which reminds me, did you bring meat?>

I ignored my infernal black hole and squinted in the darkness. I didn't see Monty or Dex, and I didn't want to start yelling out names in case Oliver had mages patrol the corridors. The air felt stale, and I couldn't sense any ambient energy around me.

<Can you sense Dex or Monty?>

<I'm sure I could locate them if they were carrying some meat.>

<Focus. Anything?>

We stood still and Peaches sniffed the air for a few seconds.

<There's nothing. Which is strange.>

<You mean you can't detect them?>

<No, I mean there's no thing here. Nothing. No magic, no scent. I can only sense you because of our bond.>

<Why does that sound familiar?>

"You're not a mage," said the female voice behind me. "What are you? How did you get in here?"

I turned to see the slim woman dressed in what could only be described as mage goth. Her hair was cropped short, almost a buzz cut. Her muscular arms flexed as she held a sharp, angry-looking serrated blade. Her clothing was black with black highlights, accessorized with darker black. It wasn't her fashion choices—questionable as they were—that stopped me cold.

She looked normal, except for her hands, which were covered in black energy—oh, and the tears. She was crying black tears.

"You're a Negomancer."

She leaped at me, blade first.

I jumped back and drew Ebonsoul in time to parry her thrust. She stepped close, pressing her body to mine.

"Your friends are dead. Stupid mages thought they could stop me. Going to kill you too."

I pushed her back and dodged a slash as she retreated

with a grin. She was fast and relentless. It was all I could do to keep her at bay. She circled me, a hungry wolf stalking prey.

Peaches growled next to me but stayed back.

<I don't hear you asking if you can bite her. This would be a good time, if you aren't too busy.>

<She has all that black stuff around her. I'm sure she tastes bad.>

<It would be helpful if you could do…something.>

<I don't want to touch her. Ugh.>

<Then do something that doesn't require you to touch her.>

<You won't like it.>

I slid to the side and made to draw Grim Whisper. She slashed at my hand, changing my mind, and spun into a back kick, burying a foot in my side with bone-crunching accuracy.

I gasped for air as the kick rearranged some internal organs and spots danced before my eyes. She came in again.

<Now would be good!>

"You were more fun than the mages, but I have to end you now." She turned her head and locked on to Peaches. "What the hell?"

I felt the buildup of energy behind us as she paused. She switched targets and ran for Peaches, but it was too late. He had been inhaling for about twenty seconds, and now he let that breath out in a bark.

I saw her ping pong against the walls as she flew a few feet down the corridor. The soundwave smacked into my chest with a thump and flung me back several feet. Immediately the corridor changed, becoming brighter.

Ahead, I could sense Dex and Monty. I leaned against the wall and caught my breath. I touched the sides of my head to make sure I wasn't bleeding. The high-pitched whine in both ears assured me my eardrums had been ruptured by my hellhound's cataclysmic bark. The familiar warm flush enveloped me as my body healed itself.

<*What the hell was that?*>

<*My bark. I told you, you wouldn't like it.*>

<*A little warning next time would be great.*>

<*I did warn you.*>

<*Telling me I won't like it isn't a warning.*>

I stood unsteadily, using the wall for balance, and headed to where I sensed Dex and Monty.

<*Did you kill her?*>

<*No, did you want me to? You just said do something. I thought you meant stop her from trying to poke you with her metal stick.*>

<*Well, that too. Thank you. Aside from making me deaf, that was pretty good.*>

<*Do I get meat now?*>

I stared at him for about five seconds before walking down the corridor. A green glow showed me where Dex was. From the scuffling and cursing, I assumed Monty was next to him.

I wondered just how powerful hellhounds were. Could he kill someone with a bark? I made a mental note to do some much needed hellhound homework when I got back home. Provided we got back home.

"She dropped on us like a pair of rank amateurs." Dex undid a black lattice that held him in place and materialized a small sausage for Peaches, who promptly hoovered it into the cavernous pit he called a stomach. I was really beginning to believe he *was* bigger on the inside.

<This is how you reward a job well done. It could be bigger, though.>

"Sorry it can't be larger. We don't want to attract any more attention. Do we, nephew?"

Monty sliced through his lattice with the walking stick.

"How was I supposed to know this damned thing would give away our position?" Monty held the stick by both ends, snapped it in two, placing it on the floor next to the Negomancer. "That should get their attention."

"TK said that thing was dangerous," I said, glancing down at the stick before turning to the Negomancer. "She was pretty stabby. Why didn't she just blast me with a black orb of doom? Isn't that what Negomancers do?"

Dex closed his eyes. "Oliver must have dampeners in place. It's not a complete lockdown, but close. Good thing we brought the pup. A few seconds more and she would have gutted you."

"Excuse me? Who was the one trapped by a lattice?"

"Trapped? We weren't trapped. I was merely biding my time and formulating a strategy until we could dispatch her."

"We walked right into a null field." Monty looked at Dex. "If it weren't for you and your creature, we'd still be in the midst of it… trapped. Thank you."

The Negomancer stirred, grabbing our attention. Peaches approached. Dex patted him on the head and moved him to one side.

<*Why do you move for him and TK, but when I try to move you, it's like moving a mountain?*>

<*I am moved…by meat. Do you make meat?*>

Dex placed a glowing green hand on her forehead, and she opened her eyes.

"What's your name, lass?"

She lashed out with a fist. Dex deflected it and twisted it past his face. With his other hand, he locked her shoulder and forced her arm into a rotation that made me wince.

"Oliver will take care of you," she said, laughing hysterically. "The others will finish you." She stopped laughing and cocked her head to one side. "I think I hear them now."

Dex held her fist and placed his hand on her forehead again. In less than a second, she was unconscious.

"We need to move, now." Monty pointed to the stairwell at the end of the corridor.

"That leads down." Dex shook his head. "We need to get to Connor and then the central chambers. That means going up."

"I know." Monty headed down the corridors. "We can take the passage though the Living Library. That will lead us to Connor, and from there, we can enter the central chamber."

"Ach, the Living Library?" Dex said. "I hate that place. Bunch of stuffed shirts with too much time to 'expound' on matters and 'posit' half-baked ideas."

"Is that the real reason?" Monty asked as we took the stairs heading down. "Or is that fear I hear in your voice, Uncle?"

The stairs were a wide spiral-winding affair. Every thirty feet, we encountered a landing. I think it was so whoever took the stairs didn't get dizzy and collapse. I looked down into the center of the staircase and couldn't see the bottom.

"How deep do they go?" I stepped back from the railing as Peaches, squeezing by me, nearly catapulted me up and over it into thin air.

"To the bottom of the Sanctuary. The Living Library is on the lowest level. From there, corridors connect to the rest of the Sanctuary."

"So are the paper dragons," Dex muttered as we took the stairs quickly. "I swear, I'll set them aflame if they get too close."

"You'll do no such thing." Monty gestured as we descended, activating runes on every landing. "They are priceless."

"What are you doing?" I asked as Monty gestured again while we passed another landing.

"I'll show you once we get to the library level."

We descended the remaining levels of the staircase in silence. Once at the bottom, Monty faced the stairs and placed his hand on the wall adjacent to the last landing.

A rune-inscribed circle dominated the center of the staircase. Monty made sure I wasn't standing on the circle as it rose. A cylinder of stone rose through the middle of the staircase, effectively removing the center.

I looked up and saw that it went all the way to the top.

"That's nice, but the staircase is still accessible. What's to stop them from just coming down—?"

Monty raised a finger. "Wait."

The landing closest to us lifted as if on a hinge and closed against the stairwell with a crash. I heard the same sound repeated up the stairs as each landing closed off the preceding staircase. Each rune-covered landing was two feet thick and made of marble.

"Never mind, even you would have a tough time getting through those slabs."

"That's the idea. It should buy us some time to investigate the library and get to Connor."

"I don't want to investigate anything." Dex scowled. "Let's get Connor and get out of here."

"We need to stop Oliver. If what Wenk said is true, we need to stop him before he consolidates his power. The other sects are in danger from his gray mages."

"I just hate this place."

Monty led us down a corridor that ended in a door twice the size of the one in the Randy Rump. I could tell it was the same material, Australian Buloke ironwood. However, this door had bands of steel running its length, in addition to being magically inscribed with runes on every inch of its surface. Some of the runes were active and remained visible. Others flashed on at intervals.

The door stood twenty feet tall and half as wide, and it put out a serious 'you shall not pass' vibe when you stood in front of it.

"Do we just knock?" I looked around at the imposing surface. "This door has seen some action."

Despite having obviously withstood enough bombardment to make the Danger Room in Fordey look newly renovated, most of the damage was superficial and cosmetic. I wondered what kind of firepower had been unleashed to cause even this much damage.

"The library has never been breached."

"If you ask me, they should just seal it and leave it sealed forever," Dex grumbled as Monty approached the enormous door. "Especially those cursed dragons."

"What's with these dragons? Why doesn't Dex like them?"

"When mages are novices, they're sent here to study the older tomes." Monty began pressing the runes on the door in sequence. "Some of the mages would try to escape their studies. Those mages, when caught—and they were *always* caught, would be assigned to the *Kyorinrin* for remedial studies."

"Damned paper dragons," Dex growled. "A good torching is what they need. Then you can send the 'Librarians' off to a dimension for the mentally damaged."

"It's been tried, more than once," Monty said with a smile. "The Kyorinrin are the embodiment of magic, and the 'Librarians' are some of the most gifted mages in the history of the Sanctuary, each a master of their discipline."

Monty pressed one last rune and stepped back.

"Which means?" I heard the immense locks scrape across stone as rumbling filled the area. While the door slowly swung open toward us, the scraping of metal was accompanied by the smell of old parchment and a cloud of dust.

"It means the Kyorinrin aren't flammable, even if they are made of paper."

A figure emerged from the dust. He was dressed casually in jeans and a long-sleeve shirt. His boots left faint impressions in the dust as he stepped forward. His sandy-brown hair was thinning on top, and he sported a goatee but no mustache.

He held a nearly transparent orb in his hand as he squinted at us. Light blue arcs traveled around his body in random patterns. They reminded me of TK and her black arcs of anger, only these arcs seemed less lethal.

He tossed the orb up and it followed him as he moved forward. Behind him, I heard the shuffling of paper but couldn't make out what was creating the noise.

"It is truly a pleasure to see you in these troubled times, Tristan, but I fear you must leave here before your presence wreaks more chaos than even we can handle."

He raised his hand to his forehead as if shielding his eyes from intense sunlight.

"You heard the man, we should go." Dex made to turn back to the spiral staircase. "Wouldn't want to bring more chaos to his door."

"Pointdexter?" the man said, still squinting. "Is that you?"

"No, it's not," Dex said and started walking away. "Don't know to whom you are referring."

"Quintus Ulberforce Alaric Niram Terrance Ulster Montague Pointdexter," the man said forcefully, his voice echoing throughout the space, "please remain where you are."

Dex froze in place as Monty and I both stared at him.

"He knows your name?" Monty asked, clearly impressed. "I thought no one knew all of your names?"

"He doesn't," Dex said, visibly upset. "He just knows enough of them to make my life miserable."

The man stepped forward but remained just inside the threshold. The rustling of paper followed him. Along with the powerful smell of old books.

"Well, it *is* a pleasure to see you, Tristan." He looked at Dex. "You, not so much. Is that a hellhound?"

"Yes, his name is Peaches." I patted him on the head and rubbed his ears.

"We don't have much information on them." He crouched down to get a closer look at Peaches. "He is exquisite."

<Do not bite him.>

<Do you think he has meat? He smells old.>

"He didn't come with a manual, unfortunately." I nudged Peaches back a good half-inch. "So far, I know he's pretty indestructible, can teleport, grow to the size of a house, and loves meat. Really loves meat."

"If you're bonded to a hellhound, you must be the chosen of Kali—Simon Strong?" He extended a hand that I shook with a look of surprise. "Don't be surprised. We may be underground, but we have many ways of getting information. We deal in knowledge. Besides, how many people do you know who walk around with a hellhound?"

"I'm afraid we may have set off the alarms." Monty looked behind us to the stairs. "We faced a Negomancer on our way here."

"Nasty business, those." He leaned over and looked behind us. "I see you've sealed off the staircase. I currently can't cross the threshold from the library or remain here for long. Are we expecting more?"

"I think so." Monty looked behind us. "Can we come in, Professor Ziller?"

He invited us in with a nod of his head. We stepped past the threshold of the enormous door, and I felt the familiar tingle of my energy signature being read. He gestured and closed the door behind us.

TWENTY-NINE

AHEAD OF US, I saw what was causing the rustling of paper.

"Don't mind the Kyorinrin, I let them roam free," Ziller said as he led us farther inside. "Are you up-to-date on your spells, Pointdexter?"

"Quite up-to-date," Dex said with a groan. "Thanks for asking."

"I can always assign one of the Kyorinrin to help you review your studies." Ziller pointed to one of the bundles of moving books. "I'm sure they'd love to help you refresh your memory, Mage Pointdexter."

"What are those?" I pointed at the shifting piles of books and scrolls.

"Kyorinrin are spirits of knowledge that are formed from ancient scrolls and books. They gather together into these dragon forms when some students disregard the priceless treasures and centuries of knowledge they contain." Ziller glanced over at Dex. "They can be tutors, where they coax students into deeper study or help them remember forgotten knowledge. If I recall, you used to call them 'paper dragons,' Mage Pointdexter."

I noticed each time Ziller said his name, Dex winced. I realized it was intentional, and for every wince, Ziller cracked a small smile. I had the feeling Dex hadn't been an ideal student.

As I looked closer at the Kyorinrin, I saw the resemblance to dragons. The Kyorinrin were decorated with ornate volumes that appeared to be a kimono. Tassels attached to scrolls hung from its head. A few of them noticed my looks and bowed in my direction. I bowed back, not wanting a scolding by a dragon made of ancient books.

"The name is Dex these days, and there's nothing wrong with my memory, thank you," Dex replied, shooting Monty a look. "This is why I didn't want to come down here."

"Dex, now?" Ziller said with a smile. "Very rugged. It suits you, Mage Pointdexter."

Monty shook his head, and I looked around as we entered the Living Library. It was about the size of the Library of Congress, multiplied ten times over. The rows appeared endless, and the presence of magic was concentrated all around us.

"What's that smell—is that the books?"

"No, these books don't age." Ziller motioned to one of the shelves. "Pick one."

I grabbed a book off the shelf and read the title: *The Weaponizing of Snark* by Mage Sturd E. Deviant. I turned a few pages, noticing that it appeared to be brand new. I lifted the book to my nose and noticed the lack of odor. Even though the date said it was over one hundred years old, it didn't smell that way. Ziller looked at my selection and smiled.

"The last student to study that book gave 'foul-mouthed' an entirely new meaning."

"It smells brand new," I said, replacing the book on the shelf.

"The smell you're getting is the biblichor from the Kyorinrin." Ziller pointed at the paper dragons shuffling behind us. "But I don't think you're here for a tour. Let's enter the Living Library."

"I thought this was the Living Library?"

Ziller shook his head, leading us to another door. It was a smaller version of the one at the entrance. "No, this area is the book repository. The Living Library is housed behind this door."

The door pulsed a faint orange. When I got closer, I realized the glow came from the runes etched into its surface. Ziller placed his hand on it, and the runes coalesced into one large rune that covered most of the door.

After a few seconds, it faded from sight, and the door returned to its previous state. He pulled it open, and we entered what appeared to be a large lounge area. Doors led off from the central area to what I guessed were sleeping quarters.

There was a dining area off to one side, with small tables situated restaurant-style next to a large counter. A few large tables in the center reminded me of every cafeteria in every school I'd ever attended.

Farther back, in a private area partitioned by a transparent wall, I could see a conference room with a large table. We made our there, walking past the center area.

"Where is everyone?" I asked, looking around.

Monty clenched his jaw at my question. "Oliver has them, doesn't he?"

"In here." Ziller pointed to the conference room. "Even now, I fear he may be able to hear us."

"How did this happen?" Monty looked around at the empty space. "Why didn't the Librarians fight back?"

"It wasn't an assault, it was a coup. Oliver planned it over years. An army of assistants was assigned to the Repository to help with the cataloguing and inventory. You saw how vast it is. We welcomed the help."

"Junior mages, I'm assuming?" Monty asked.

"When he demanded the Librarians surrender, we organized, prepared to launch an attack. By that time, his gray mages were in place."

"The army of assistants was a real army." Dex added, "Probably battle mages in training."

"We didn't see it coming. He threatened to destroy the repository," Ziller said, shaking his head. "The Librarians felt they had no choice. They may be mages, but they're not battle mages. They're scholars at heart. A few of us decided we wouldn't surrender the Repository. This meant we needed a plan."

"They surrendered," Monty said, "and gave him access to millennia of knowledge, but hid you in the library."

Ziller nodded. "He wouldn't harm the Living Library, or so we thought, but we couldn't let him have access to the tomes of the Repository. It's the largest of all the sects."

"The knowledge contained here would make him

unstoppable."

"I needed time to get my calculations correct." Ziller gestured and created another transparent orb. It flickered and solidified, giving us a view of the staircase. "One of the Librarians masked me and created a simulacrum with my essence."

"An observation orb," Monty said, looking at the floating orb. "You used these to monitor the situation?"

"More like spy on mages minding their own business," Dex muttered under his breath. "Those things are an invasion of privacy."

"I used to use them to keep track of young mages with a propensity for unimaginable destruction." Ziller looked at Monty and Dex. Both managed to look away at that moment. "But, yes, the orbs helped me to monitor the Sanctuary."

"You hide here, and then what?" I looked around. "Call the cavalry?" I didn't see where he was going.

"They found the simulacrum," Monty said.

Ziller looked away. "Do you remember Professor Baudri?"

"Not fondly, his classes were the most difficult. He taught simulacra and simulation. It was a nightmare, both real and imagined."

"He created my double, imbued it with my essence, and fooled everyone—even Oliver. He paid for it with his life."

"He bought you time," Monty said. "To figure out the projections."

"My discipline and strength is quantum runic mechanics, but even I hadn't tried something like this." Ziller shook his head. "By the time Oliver came for me and the Repository, I had simply shifted the entire library."

"You what? What do you mean you 'shifted' the library?" I looked at the stunned Monty, who only stared straight ahead before answering.

"The entire library?" Monty asked quietly. "Wait, you *knew* I was coming?"

"Yes, I recognized your signature, Tristan, as you activated the landings on the way down the staircase."

"I didn't open the door, did I?" Monty looked at Ziller. "Even with the sequence."

"No, the door can't be opened without my energy signature, like you saw earlier. Right now, we're at the Sanctuary, but we aren't."

"This is Schrödinger's cat taken to an extrapolatory tangent with, with—"

I'd never seen Monty at a loss for words.

"With a bit of Zeno effect and runic constancy to propel the state changes," Ziller finished. "It's quite amazing, actually. I didn't think it would work, but the theory was sound, and well, here we are—or aren't."

"It means you can't leave," Dex said after a moment. "Or you lose the library."

Ziller smiled as if Dex had just aced a test. "I see you remember your quantum runic compression."

"Lose the library?" I looked at Monty, who still seemed to be in a mild state of shock. "How can you lose the entire library?"

"The Repository, yes. The others felt this was the only way to keep the books safe from Oliver and his mages." Ziller looked down at his crossed hands. "If I cross the threshold, the library can be thrown into flux and lost. I'm the anchor point, keeping it fixed in this and several other potentialities."

"What's to stop Oliver from shutting you down and finding the library in the Sanctuary he's in?" I asked, confused as to how we were at the Sanctuary but also not there.

"He would need a master quantum runic mathematician to figure out the paths, which are infinite at this point." Ziller looked up at me. "In addition, he would need to find a mage strong enough to form the runes that would allow interstitial planar travel on an unprecedented scale. I only know one person who can do that."

"You," I said, understanding the play. "You didn't escape."

"Escape? No, I didn't escape. I sealed the Repository, but Oliver isn't interested only in the books."

"He needs your knowledge to fulfill his plan." Monty rubbed his chin. "He plans to take over the other sects and usher in a new age of magic. For that, he needs to place his mages without the sects or humanity being aware of what's happening. He needs quantum magic."

"He's mad. Magic-users will be wiped off the face of the earth if he attempts that. And it won't stop there."

"He'll try what he did with the library. He'll place his gray mages in key positions, and when he feels the time is right, he'll strike from within. The gray mages can hide their signatures, can't they?"

"It's how we missed them in the library." Ziller nodded. "They can mask and appear like low-level mages, even normals."

"He's using the Librarians to create the gray mages,

isn't he?" Dex asked. "With their knowledge…"

"It's the only thing that makes sense," Ziller agreed. "Oliver alone can't do it, but with the Living Library, he doesn't have to."

"How many mages make up this Living Library?" I wondered how many hostages Oliver held.

"There are seven of us…well, six now, with Baudri gone."

"Why don't the Librarians bolt or revolt or something? The books are safe. They can just cast a circle and get out of here."

"The Sanctuary is on a minimal energy signature. Which means Oliver controls energy expenditure, how much and by whom. He's using dampeners."

Monty looked around the library. "How are you managing the energy requirements if you're in a constant state of flux?"

"I'm using quantum tunneling to pick up excess infrared and runic nanogens to divert the ambient energy given off by the Repository and channel it into the shifts."

Monty tapped his chin. "Do you have any of these runic nanogens available?"

Ziller handed Monty a flat disc about the size of a quarter.

"What about the others? The Elders?"

"Oliver turned or erased the Elders who stood against him. Except for your father, Tristan. He needs Connor, or rather his essence."

"His essence?" Monty looked confused. "Why would he need my father's essence? They're almost at the same level of power."

"How strong do you think your father is?" Ziller asked. "Do you know? How long has it been since you've seen him, and I don't mean through a Smith Bridge."

"I know he's a few shifts away from becoming Archmage," Monty started.

Ziller shook his head. "That would be Oliver. Connor isn't a few shifts away."

"A shift?"

"Connor Montague has been an Archmage for over a year now."

"An Archmage? My father? How?"

"Connor is exceptionally gifted, even among the Elders." Ziller looked into the observation orb. "We had been investigating quantum shifts, trying a radical permutation to unlock an easier path to the shifts."

"That's impossible. There aren't any shortcuts to shifting higher." Monty slammed a hand on the table. "No one has managed it, ever."

"He unlocked it," Ziller said quietly. "Connor figured out the permutation. Even I don't know how he did it."

"That's my brother, stubborn as a mule." Dex shook his head. "If I know Connor, he felt it was too dangerous to share...upset the balance?"

Ziller looked over at Dex. "Oliver found out and wanted it. Connor refused, saying exactly that...it was too dangerous. It would place too much power in the hands of the unprepared. Before I knew it, Connor was imprisoned, and the Librarians were being taken."

"Why doesn't Connor blast Oliver with his Archmageness?" I looked around the table. "He has the power."

"Because Oliver is holding the one thing that can stop Connor, even with the power of an Archmage." Ziller glanced at Monty and then looked at me again.

"Is there some kind of Archmage kryptonite I'm not familiar with?"

"He has it, doesn't he?" Monty asked. "It's the only way."

"Yes, Connor believes Oliver is holding Sara Montague's essence within him."

THIRTY

DEX LOOKED AT Monty and stood. "We need to get to Connor." His voice was hard as his jaw flexed.

"It's suicide," Ziller said, standing. "He's being held in the central chamber, surrounded by gray mages and Oliver."

"I know my brother. He'll never give Oliver his essence, even if it means setting Sara free."

Monty nodded. "My uncle's right. How can we access the central chamber from here?"

"You can't," Ziller replied. "If he gets a hold of you in this condition..." He narrowed his eyes at Monty, who looked away. "Did you really think I wouldn't notice the reservoirs or your diminished signature?"

"This is temporary." Monty looked down at the rings on his fingers. "I'll regain my casting and my defenses."

"He's using Connor as a conduit. Do you know what that means if he captures you?"

"What does that mean, a conduit?" I asked.

"Blood relatives share special bonds, very much like you and your creature. The closer the relative, the closer the bond."

"Peaches and I are *not* related." I looked down at the slumbering mass of canine destruction lying at my feet. "At least I don't think we are. Can you do the Vulcan mindspeak with your father?"

"I've never been close to Father. He's always kept his mind guarded, even from me. It's been known to happen in times of stress, though. I suppose, theoretically, it's possible."

"I think Peaches and I share a different kind of bond. His thoughts are mostly meat-related."

"But you are bonded," Dex added. "And we know what happens if that bond is broken."

"So you're saying if Oliver kills Connor, Monty becomes a supersized, monster mage?"

Monty turned and stared, giving me the 'did you slam your head against the wall?' look. "Are you serious?"

"If Oliver kills Tristan, he can extract information from Connor during the severing. In his current condition, Tristan's defenses wouldn't be strong enough to stop him. Connor would be an open book."

"Oliver would get the permutation," I said, connecting the dots. "He would become an Archmage."

"And proceed to take over the sects." Monty looked down at his hands and made a fist. I noticed he was down to eight rings out of the ten, and one of the rings was light gray.

"You inhaled obsidian ice, Tristan. You may never recover your ability to cast."

"I know."

"And you think you, your uncle, and your immortal friend with his hellhound are going to stop a group of trained mages?" Ziller asked, throwing his hands up in the air and bumping the observation orb out of the way. "You're more insane than Oliver."

"I have to try."

"You always were stubborn." Ziller looked at Dex. "Do you remember the Void Passage? Follow me."

Dex winced. "I thought that was sealed after last time."

Ziller led us out of the conference room, down a narrow corridor, and into a small room about twice the size of a broom closet. He opened the door and motioned for us to enter, closing the door as he followed behind us.

"It was sealed after you and your friends traversed it, after being given explicit instructions not to do so."

Ziller placed a hand on the back wall, revealing another door like the one at the entrance of the Living Library.

"I created this one in case we ever needed a way into the central chamber." Ziller placed his hand on the door, opening it. "I never thought we would need it for this."

"Anyone going to explain this Void Passage? Can we start with how long it is?"

"As long or as short as you make it," Ziller replied. "It's a test designed for mages to face their worst fears. The physical passage runs through the center of the Sanctuary, about eight hundred meters long. From here, you would be halfway through the passage. It had to be sealed after it drove several novices mad."

"Mad, as in crazy? Not mad as in angry?"

"Mad, as in drooling, gibbering mages who didn't

even remember who they were and who tried to gnaw through their own fingers to stop the screaming."

I turned to Monty. "And we're taking this passage because…?"

"It's for mages, you should be safe."

"Those sound like famous last words."

"True," Ziller said with a nod. "If it does begin to affect you, remember, it's better to run toward your fear rather than away from it."

"You've crossed the passage." Ziller looked at Dex. "You can get them across."

"That was a long time ago," Dex replied, shaking his head. "I was young, reckless and more than a bit foolish."

"This time you aren't so young." Ziller grabbed him by the arm. "Whatever you do, you can't let Connor give Oliver the permutation. I don't know how he got Sara's essence, or if it's really hers. What matters is that Connor believes it's hers."

"I'll stop him," Dex said, his face grim. "No matter what."

Dex stepped through the door and disappeared. Monty was about to go through when Ziller stopped him. "It's not Sara. No matter what you think you see or hear, it's not your mother. Do you understand?"

"I do."

"You can't do this on your own. Rely on those around you."

Monty remained silent for a few seconds. "We'll stop Oliver and get my father back." He stepped through and followed Dex.

"Are you sure this is the only way to the central

chamber?"

"Positive," he answered, and pointed to my chest. "You're a shieldbearer. Nana?"

I nodded and reflexively put my hand to the pendant. "She said it's Monty's."

"It is, but he's not quite ready for it. He's a Montague, this means he's going to burn through those rings and he'll jury-rig the runic nanogen to give him more power."

"I don't know how to help or stop him," I said. "It's like he wants to die."

"He's not himself after the ice. You have to do the hardest thing you will ever find yourself doing. You have to let him get to zero. He has to hit bottom."

"What if Oliver attacks him?"

"There's no if. Oliver will attack him. It's the only way to sever the bond."

"I can't stand against Oliver. He's some super-psycho, crazy mage."

"It's not your job to stand against him. Your job is to stand beside Tristan," he answered. "What do you think shieldbearers are for?"

I was about to step through the door, when a question grabbed me. Peaches rammed into my leg, nearly knocking me down as I stopped suddenly.

I turned to face Ziller. "Before I go and face my imminent death and/or brain melting, can you tell me why mages speak the way they do?"

"What do you mean?" He looked at me innocently. "We're understanding each other right now, aren't we?"

"Every time Monty tries to explain something magical or otherworldly, he starts with one of your 'theorems' and then proceeds to destroy my neurons with some insane explanation based on your work."

"That's a good point." Ziller rubbed his chin. "I can only tell you what I was taught."

"What?" I asked, getting ready to step through the door.

"Sometimes, a spoon is just a spoon, and sometimes it's a construct comprised of a dual nature, being simultaneously concave, convex and utilized for the displacement of food."

"That's your answer, really?"

He laughed and gently pushed me forward. "No, it's yours."

I stepped into the darkness with Peaches next to me as the door vanished.

THIRTY-ONE

I STOOD IN a featureless stone corridor. Up ahead, I saw Dex and Monty examining the runes on one of the walls as they walked forward. Peaches nudged my leg as I tried to pinpoint where the corridor ended.

"I can't believe you crossed this passage." Monty shook his head as he followed Dex down the corridor. "I thought that was impossible."

"Improbable is not the same as impossible, nephew. You of all people should know that."

<Hold on a second, boy, I'm trying to find where the corridor ends.>

<Meat.>

A dim light illuminated the area where we stood, but it became darker as I looked farther down the corridor. I walked ahead, trying to catch up to them.

"I'll ask Dex to make you some in a second, you black hole. Give me a moment to orient—"

The growl stopped me short. Was there something in the corridor I couldn't see? I turned to look behind us, and I saw it. Peaches stood squarely in the center of the corridor. His eyes were glowing red, and he was growling…at me.

<Meat.>

<Hey, boy, what's wrong? I'll get you meat later. Let's catch up to Monty and Dex.>

No response.

The runes on the sides of his body exploded with light. He opened his mouth and drool spilled onto the floor. The growling dropped a few octaves and he gnashed his teeth.

"Oh, shit." I opened my jacket, giving me access to Ebonsoul. "Calm down, boy. Is this crazy corridor affecting you? Monty! Dex!"

I stole a quick glance behind me, but they were gone. I turned back at the sound of another growl.

"Boy, you need to calm down now. We can get out of here. It's me, Simon, your bondmate."

He lowered his head and charged. I drew Ebonsoul and raised my arm to block him. He jumped in the air and blinked out. He reappeared behind me and sank his fangs into my thigh before blinking out again.

Agony shot up my leg as my body flushed hot, trying to repair the damage. Blood was flowing from the wound. I put my back against the wall to limit his angles of attack.

"Shit, shit, shit," I muttered as my leg grew slick with blood—my blood. "Don't do this, boy. It's me, Simon."

He blinked in mid-leap in front of me, jaws going for my throat. I raised my arm reflexively and buried Ebonsoul in his chest. The blade immediately siphoned his life and flooded me with a rush of power.

"No! No!" I yelled. "Oh no, please stop, stop." I

tossed Ebonsoul to the side, and he fell into my arms. We fell to the floor, his tongue lolling to one side. Blood flowed from his wound and his mouth as his breathing became ragged. He looked up at me. His eyes weren't glowing, and the runes along the sides of his body had gone dark.

<Why? Why did you poke me with the metal stick? I only wanted some...>

His head rolled to the side. I knelt in shock, holding his body.

"Simon! Run!" Monty yelled behind me. I looked up to see an orb punch through his shoulder as a group of mages ran down the corridor.

"What? How?" I looked down at my blood-soaked hands.

Behind him, Dex ran as he blasted green orbs at the mages chasing them. "Move! Simon! Get up, boy!"

I got to my feet, and Monty shoved me forward as he cast a lattice behind us. He spit up blood as he gestured. We ran down the corridor as orbs blasted the walls next to us, narrowly missing our heads.

"What happened? What happened!" I tried to process what was going on. Orbs crashed into the wall next to us, splintering the stone.

"We could use some help. Where's your creature?"

"Peaches turned on me. He tried to attack me!"

"They must have done something to the passage." He cast another lattice behind the first one. "The gray mages are too strong. There are too many of them."

"What are you saying? Are we aborting? What about your father?"

"What do you bloody think I'm saying? We're no

match for them. We underestimated Oliver. He's too strong. This mission was doomed from the start."

I looked at his hands. "You're down to one ring. You have to stop, Monty."

"What were we thinking," he mumbled to himself. "This plan was a bloody nightmare from the inception. You have to go, Simon, you still have a chance. Get back to the door."

He cast another lattice and created several orbs of flame. He unleashed the orbs and formed three more.

"Stop, Monty!" I drew Grim Whisper and fired at the incoming mages, but my bullets disintegrated before they reached them.

I saw the lattices fade from sight as the last ring became dust around his finger. A barrage of black orbs raced down the corridor and punched through his body, slamming and bouncing him along the wall. His mangled body slid down into a seated position, leaving a bloody trail on the wall behind him as he dropped to the floor.

"Run," he gasped. "Go back to the door."

His lifeless eyes stared back at me as a black orb punched into the wall next to my head.

"Monty! No! Fuck, no!" I raced to his body, as an arm grabbed me and pulled me back. A slap brought me back to my senses and Dex got in my face, shaking me by both arms.

"Lad! What are you, a target? Get moving, he's gone!" Dex shoved me forward. He ran behind me as we made our way back to the door. Another barrage of black orbs narrowly missed us as he turned. Covered in green, he gestured, unleashing a wave of green energy behind us.

The wave raced along the floor, blasting and disintegrating the front line of mages. The rest leaped over the green wave and unleashed a barrage of angry black orbs.

Dex placed his hands together and looked back at me.

"Run!" He faced the oncoming mages and spread his arms wide. A blast of green energy shot forward. The gray mages threw up a wall and deflected the blast. Two gray mages gestured as the third slid forward with a black orb.

The orb raced at Dex and enveloped him in a black lattice. He screamed as it started dissolving him.

"Run, lad!" Dex yelled as a gray mage stepped forward and buried a sword in his chest. He fell forward and became dust as the lattice undid his body. A green blast filled the corridor, blinding me. When I could see again, the gray mages were gone.

"They trusted you and paid with their lives." The voice drifted over to where I stood and caressed the nape of my neck like a blade. She was behind me. "They should have known better."

I turned and faced the one responsible for everything.

"I told you, everything and everyone you love will perish. Then, you will seek death and not find it. You will long to die, but death will escape you. At that time, our paths will cross again."

It was Kali.

THIRTY-TWO

I FELL TO my knees, my bloody hands empty. Tears were flowing down my cheeks. I knew she was right. They had trusted me, and I betrayed them. Before me stood the proof.

Kali the Destroyer.

Her chocolate skin glistened in the dim light of the corridor. She wore a simple black dress that hung from her body. Her long black hair hung loose, and it appeared to have a life of its own as it flowed around her in the non-existent wind.

I felt a gnawing, burning grief that wanted to swallow me whole. I wanted to scream until I couldn't scream anymore, and then I wanted to scream some more. My mouth was ash. I tried to form the words but found I couldn't.

My body sagged in defeat under her gaze. I only saw death in her eyes, and then she smiled. I smiled back because I knew soon it would be over.

"Hello, my chosen one." She reached down and raised my face with a finger under my chin. "It's time to end this wretched existence of yours."

Her skin was cool to the touch, and she smelled like fresh earth. She smiled down at me as I nodded. I felt no fear, only relief. It washed over me. It would all be over soon.

No fear.

She produced Ebonsoul and presented it to me.

"Take it, my chosen one. Finish it."

"You know what? I think I'm going to give you that honor," I said, my voice a jagged rasp. "I mean, you did curse me. Why not let you be the one to end it?"

She stepped back and gazed at me. "No, my chosen. This is your privilege. Accept it."

"Pass," I said, getting to my feet. "Let me guess what happens: I take the 'blade' and go samurai seppuku, and my brain is fried oatmeal. Am I close?"

"To death, if you do not obey my command," she said, her voice echoing through the chamber. "Do it now!"

I raised an eyebrow at the impressive acoustics.

"No. You screwed up," I said, shaking my head. "Yes, I'm scared of losing those closest to me. But that's not my greatest or worst fear."

She stepped back as I took the blade. As I suspected, it disappeared once I grabbed hold of the hilt.

"I command you, chosen one."

"Give it a rest, you're not Kali. Not even close."

"You will never escape this place."

"I already have."

She faded into black smoke and disappeared. I felt a wetness slap me across the face. I looked up at the ginormous, slobbering face of my hellhound. Peaches looked down and slapped me with his tongue again as I pushed him away.

<Your tongue-fu is strong, but stop licking me.>

<What is tongue-fu? Is it a kind of meat? Can I have some?>

<No—yes, I'll ask Dex.>

<My saliva cured you. I told you it has healing properties. You can thank me later…with meat.>

He gave me another lick before moving to the side for Monty. I noticed he still had eight rings on his fingers and I breathed a sigh of relief.

"Simon?" Monty asked as I opened my eyes in the corridor. "Welcome back. You crossed the passage."

"You're still alive." I blinked against the bright light of the green orb Dex held. "Both of you are."

"Last I checked. Did you hit your head against the floor? One moment you're walking behind us, the next you collapsed."

"He's fine. Daft as usual." Dex grunted as he stood up. "How was your trip down the passage?"

"I thought it only worked on mages?" I rubbed my head as the pain of a headache squeezed my brains flat and did an Irish jig over them, with steel-toed combat boots.

"Seems you're abnormal, but I guessed that early on since you were running with my nephew," Dex said. "Didn't think you were *that* abnormal."

"How long have I been out?"

"Ten minutes." Dex made his way down the corridor with Peaches next to him.

"Ten minutes?" I looked at Monty, who nodded. "Felt much longer than that."

"What do you remember? Did you face your fear?"

"Too much. Yes, and no. My brain is still fuzzy." I got to my feet and leaned against the wall as the curse started kicking in, and my body flushed with heat. "I'll be good in a few minutes."

Dex walked back to where we stood.

"Well, begging your pardon, kind sirs. If you feel up to it, we need to find and stop a deranged mage intent on causing global destruction, and free your father—my brother. Think you can fit that into your busy schedule?"

"Give me a minute." I rested my head against the cool wall. "This is called recovering."

"Would you like a pillow, maybe a cup of coffee?"

I glared at Dex, who gave me a short bow. "The hilarity runs strong in your family."

"The end of the world waits for no one." He looked at Monty. "Do you remember the layout of this place?'

Monty looked behind us and gave him a short nod. "It's been a while, but this configuration looks familiar."

"It should, you ran it enough when you were younger. Get yourself oriented."

Monty closed his eyes and turned in a slow circle. After a complete revolution, he stopped and opened his eyes.

"This is the interior of the central structure. The Void Passage brought us just past the cruciform galleries?"

"Correct." Dex swiped the side of his nose at him. "We have two courtyards to cross and a hell of a lot of stairs to climb before we get to the main chamber."

"Any chance these courtyards will be empty?"   I

checked Grim Whisper and loaded persuader rounds, making sure I had extra magazines. Ebonsoul was secure in its runed sheath.

"About the same odds of your pup becoming vegetarian," Dex said with a grin. He stepped to a large door resembling the one that had sealed off the library.

"Are we still in the passage?" I asked Monty, who had stepped next to me. I noticed my hands still had micro tremors as I grabbed the holster holding Grim Whisper.

I held my hand up and the tremors slowly disappeared. I moved the entropy magazines to another pocket for easy loading. I reached for my flask and took a long pull of Valhalla Java.

If I was going to face a mage intent on taking us out, I was going to have Valkyrie coffee in my veins while he tried it. The effect was immediate, as my senses and reflexes ratcheted up to overdrive.

"No," Monty replied slowly as he watched me drink. "Should you be drinking so much of that?"

"What's it going to do, kill me?" I wiped my mouth with the back of my hand and then replaced the flask inside my jacket. "So this isn't the passage?"

"Good point. The passage transports you to the other side of the Sanctuary once you cross. Were you thinking of crossing it again?"

The images of them dying flashed before my eyes.

"Not for as long as I live. In fact, we don't even need to discuss it again, ever."

"That is the usual response, from what I've heard," he said with a short nod and adjusted the sleeves of his jacket. "We may not walk away from this one. Ready?"

"No, but when has that stopped us?"

THIRTY-THREE

DEX REARRANGED THE runes on the door, made us step back, formed a large green orb, and launched it at the door. He gestured and cast a wall of energy between the door and us.

"Dex, I think those doors are designed to withstand magical attacks—"

The orb glided up to the door and stopped just short. I looked on in confusion.

"Wait for it," he said, holding up a hand. "Runic doors take a little coaxing."

The orb flowed into the door and disappeared. The next second, all of the runes shifted to green. Cracks appeared in the door, with green light shining through them. I felt the shift in energy as the door exploded. Shards of wood and metal flew by us, embedding themselves in the ground and walls.

We walked through the doorway and saw the bodies of gray mages littering the courtyard entrance. Some of them moaned and groaned. All of them had injuries. None of them tried to move against us.

The rectangular courtyard was enclosed with columns on four sides, forming corridors between them and the walls. The old stone glimmered with runes and ambient power.

Alcoves lined each wall every few feet, each of them covered with runes and ornate stone work. Four tiered stone towers, one on every corner of the courtyard, enclosed the space.

The center of the courtyard was dominated by a larger tiered stone tower covered in black runes and soaring twice as high as the corner towers.

"If that's coaxing, I don't want to see you apply force." I looked at the faces of the mages. Most of them appeared to be in their late twenties or early thirties. "They must have been standing too close to the door."

"Inner guard," Monty said, pointing with his chin. "Incoming."

I ducked behind a column as a barrage of flame orbs tried to incinerate me. I drew Grim Whisper and peeked around the column I was using for cover. I counted several dozen mages dressed in gray robes. All of them looked eager to barbecue us.

"Just how many of these mages does Oliver have?"

"The Golden Circle is one of the largest and oldest sects." Monty cast an orb around a column. It weaved around the stone pillar and slammed into an unsuspecting group of mages, knocking them unconscious. "He could have anywhere from one hundred to three hundred novices in the grounds."

"Three hundred mages?"

"Not all of them would have agreed to follow

Oliver's madness."

"Faced with erasure, young mages would choose to follow," Dex snapped as he caught a few orbs and tossed them back to their owners, blasting them into the walls with force. "Maybe you should let the pup out to play?"

Peaches nudged me and nearly pushed me into a group of flame orbs that blasted the wall.

<Can I bite them?>

<I don't know. These guys want to bake us.>

<With fire?>

I remembered the images of the passage and shrugged them off, shaking my head. Part of me wanted him to stay close where I could keep him safe. Then I remembered he was a hellhound; he was the one keeping me safe.

<Be careful. Bite them, but don't get hit by the orbs.>

<Bite them carefully? How do I do that?>

<Can you stop them without biting them?>

<I could tap them with my head and paws?>

I'd felt his 'taps' and almost felt sorry for the gray mages.

<Tap away.>

He leaped into the courtyard and blinked out. I heard a bone-crunching thud followed by a strangled scream as he pounced on a gray mage and went to work on another. Some of the mages focused on Peaches, and I dropped them with Persuaders.

Monty stepped from behind the column and unleashed an onslaught of tiny blue orbs about the size of marbles. They punched into the mages and knocked them off their feet, covering them in blue energy. He gestured, and the remaining mages, not stomped on by Peaches, convulsed on the ground.

"Shockers." Dex grinned as he tossed small discs at the incapacitated mages. "I remember when I taught you that spell."

"I'm sure most, if not all, of them can be rehabilitated." Monty led the way past the incapacitated mages. "Erasure is a frightening option at any age."

"Aye, you sound like Connor." Dex nodded and wiped the sweat off his brow. With a gesture, the discs flared bright green, and the mages disappeared. "Besides, it's not the novices that worry me."

"Where did you send them?" I looked at the empty courtyard. "That is a handy spell."

"Aye, it is, and costly too." Dex was looking a little worse for wear as he caught his breath. "I sent them someplace safe."

"The Elders could have fought back, but perhaps Oliver moved against them the same way he did with the library? By the time they realized what was happening, it would've been too late."

"People are intelligent, mobs aren't." I holstered Grim Whisper as Peaches blinked in next to my leg. "I think the Elders, after centuries of having it, probably found it harder to let go of power than these mages. Maybe he promised them even more?"

"They betrayed the Sanctuary," Dex said, flexing the muscles of his jaw. "They should have died or been erased before joining him or accepting any offers of power."

"Power tends to corrupt," I said.

"And absolute power corrupts absolutely," Monty

answered as he led the way up.

We climbed the stairs to the central tower and stood in front of a pair of rune-covered black doors that glistened in the sunlight. They were larger than the library door and radiated an oppressive malignant energy.

Unlike the library door, which informed you that it was foolish to attempt to open it, the vibe from these doors was more along the lines of 'please try and open us so we can crush you like the bug that you are and laugh while we do it.' For a second, I considered the airstrike option.

"Oliver takes his security seriously. Where did he get these, Mordor Exteriors and Doors?" I went to place a hand on one of the doors, and Dex yanked my arm back, nearly dislocating my shoulder as he shook his head.

"What?"

"These"—he narrowed his eyes at the imposing slabs of wood and metal as he pushed me back—"are Suicide Doors. You don't want to go touching them, even being immortal."

Peaches whined next to me and backed up.

A crack of thunder made me jump, as arcs of white energy leaped off the four smaller towers around us. Each of the arcs struck the main center tower, making the stone and the doors glow with white runes.

I looked up at the doors. "Dex, you don't happen to have another one of those door exploders, do you?"

"Ach. For one of my 'door exploders'—as you call them—to work, I have to rearrange the runes on the door and exploit the weakness. I can't even touch this door."

Monty gestured, and I noticed he was down to six rings.

"What are you doing?" I pointed at the rings. "You have to save those. Dex?"

"He can't breach these doors using his life force. Besides, he doesn't know the spell." Monty kept gesturing and retrieved the runic nanogen Ziller had given him.

"How do you know a spell I don't?" Dex crossed his arms and glared. "I taught you all the spells you know."

"Not all of them. You need to get safe, now."

Monty kept gesturing as Dex's eyes widened. The sixth ring faded to gray on Monty's finger, and he kept gesturing.

"Bloody hell." Dex grabbed me by the arm and led me down the stairs. From the bottom of the stairs, I saw a black cloud envelop Monty and hide him from view.

"What is that?"

"We need shelter." Dex looked around as if trying to find a good place to hide. "And quick."

"From what?" I kept my gaze fixed on the dark area in front of the doors. "What the hell is that?"

Dex snapped his fingers. "Your shield. Over here, hurry."

"What is that?"

He led us to one of the alcoves in the wall behind the columns. The alcoves were deep enough to hold all three of us if we squeezed in. Peaches huddled by our feet as Dex gestured.

"Get your shield up." He wiped the sweat out of his

eyes. "Hurry, before he lets that thing go."

I pressed the main bead on the mala, and the shield materialized in front of us. Dex grabbed the edge of the shield and whispered something under his breath. A green wave flowed into it, making it larger and curved, covering the entire alcove.

"He's using too much energy." I looked to where the black cloud of energy pulsed. "At this rate, he's going to burn through all the reservoirs. He won't have anything left to face Oliver."

"I don't think he's worried about that too much at the moment."

"What are you talking about?"

"Where in bloody hell did he learn a dark corsolis?" Dex squinted through the shield. "I never even taught him a regular corsolis, much less a dark one. This must be the work of that sorceress he's sweet on."

"Roxanne?" I shook my head. "No, he learned the corsolis at his last shift. I was there when he faced Beck and exploded an entire level…. Oh, shit."

"Figured it out, have you?" Dex kept his gaze fixed on Monty. "Whatever you do, don't let your shield drop."

THIRTY-FOUR

ANOTHER CRACK OF thunder filled the courtyard, and a black wave of energy descended from the center tower.

"Avert your eyes!" Dex yelled as he turned my head and looked away. I made sure Peaches' eyes were covered, even though I didn't know what effect the spell would have on a hellhound. The wave slammed into the shield, rocking us. It was the sound of an angry ocean, roaring and threatening to rip us out of the alcove as the energy battered the enhanced shield.

After a few seconds, silence embraced the courtyard. I pressed the mala bead and dropped the shield. The floor of the courtyard was a scorched ruin. The entire courtyard looked like ground zero to a runic, nuclear bomb.

Everywhere I looked, the stone was cracked and scorched. All of the columns had suffered damage, some of them missing entirely. One of the four corner towers had collapsed, and the other three were scorched and missing sections.

I looked up the stairs but didn't see Monty. The Suicide Doors had been blasted apart. I raced up the stairs with Peaches keeping pace. We reached the top and I saw Monty on one knee. Blood poured from his nose and the side of his mouth. I saw his hand and counted four rings left. He wiped the blood away and gave me a nod as he stood slowly.

"I could really use a cup of tea." He looked into the charred entrance of the center tower. "That was harder than I thought it would be, even with the runic nanogen."

I patted my jacket, pulled out my skull-covered flask, and handed it to him. He examined it, reluctantly at first, and then took a deep pull of what I guess was, for him, Valhalla Earl Grey.

"That was refreshing." He handed me the flask and shrugged out of his suit jacket. "Thank you."

His suit jacket was torn and ragged as he removed it and placed it on the floor beside him. Small blisters had formed on his hands and face. He gestured and a soft golden light enveloped the burned areas.

"Are you bloody daft?" Dex yelled, climbing the last of the stairs and gasping. "A dark corsolis? Where did you learn—when did you learn that spell?"

Monty motioned to the doors. Dex grabbed his hand, eyeing the remaining four rings. Monty removed his hand slowly. "We needed to get inside, and it was the only way."

"Not if it means losing you, boy. There's always a choice."

Monty turned to enter the tower, when I felt an energy shift. For a split second, the memory of the passage raced in my mind. I looked as Peaches growled and entered 'shred and crush' mode. He was looking at the entrance of the tower. Inside the tower was an open space. Residual arcs of dark energy danced along the floor. The interior was dim, making it hard to see all the details.

"There's only one choice and it lies inside." Monty stepped into the tower.

"Monty, wait—" I started, as a blast of black energy hit him squarely in the chest and launched him across the courtyard.

<Go get him, boy!>

Peaches blinked out and reappeared mid-air next to Monty. He clamped on to his arm and blinked out again. They both reappeared behind the columns. I saw Monty get to his feet, using the wall for support. He coughed and spat blood as he looked in my direction, giving me a nod.

<That deserves extra meat.>

<One extra-large sausage for you. Stay next to him, boy. Keep him safe.>

I moved to the side and looked into the tower. My eye caught the movement of a figure approaching us from across the floor. Behind the figure, suspended horizontally several feet off the floor in a mid-air spread eagle, was Connor Montague. I switched out the magazine and loaded entropy rounds.

Black bands of energy were attached to his arms, legs and neck, keeping him in place. On the floor beneath him, I saw five figures standing in the center of a large circle, gesturing. Black tendrils of energy shot up from the circle and embedded themselves in Connor's body.

I moved back down the stairs, fighting an overwhelming wall of force pressed against me. Dex grunted next to me as he tried to resist but found himself backing down with me.

We were forced back to the courtyard floor as the figure emerged from the tower into the sun. For a moment, he closed his eyes, ignoring us, and faced the light, basking in the rays.

He wore a simple black Armani suit with a black Brooks Brothers shirt and a Zegna tie made of gold silk. A pair of black Isaias finished the ensemble, and I wondered if maybe he and Hades were shopping buddies.

His gray hair was cut short and parted on one side. If he ever decided megalomaniacal mage didn't work, he could always model for a living.

He looked down the stairs. I saw violet energy race across his eyes and realized the nightmare had officially begun. The voice in my head suggested that this would be the best time for the airstrike, particularly if I were standing directly under it when it hit. I took a step back, fully intending to run and not stop until I arrived at a minimal safe distance, like Antarctica.

The fear must have shown in my expression because Dex grabbed my shoulder and squeezed hard enough for me to wince.

"It's poor form to blast open a door when a knock would've sufficed," the man said from the top of the stairs. "Do you know how difficult it was to install those doors? I lost at least thirty or forty mages in the process."

Dex formed fists with his hands. "I'm going to enjoy

watching you die, Oliver."

"No, I don't think so, old man. Here's what's going to happen: I'm going to offer Tristan over there a choice. If he refuses, I'll put him out of his misery, severing the Montague bond. Connor, in there"—he thumbed behind him—"is going to give me the permutation. Then, I'm going to put the rest of you down. After that, maybe lunch."

"You bastard, let my brother go."

I drew Grim Whisper, and Oliver raised an eyebrow.

"You are so far out of your depth, Mr. Strong, you can't fathom the power you're facing. I would try explaining it to you, but your poor brain would probably melt in the process."

"I get that a lot. Let Connor go."

"And then what, repent of my ways? Allow them to perform an erasure? Imprisoned for the rest of my days? Forgive me if I decline."

"A swift death will suit me just fine," Dex growled and began to gesture, his hands glowing green.

"Are you posing, or do you intend to shoot?" Oliver asked, staring at me and ignoring Dex.

I emptied the magazine. Oliver raised a hand, stopping the bullets mid-flight and pulling off a Neo in my face. Except my rounds didn't fall to the ground. He waved a finger around and flicked his fingers forward. I barely pressed my mala bead in time before all of the rounds pounded into my shield.

"A shield—how quaint." He slashed his arm across his body and I flew across the courtyard, slamming into a few columns along the way before crashing into a wall face-first, cratering it. "I'll be right with you, Mr. Strong.

Don't go anywhere."

My body blasted heat as it dealt with several broken bones and critical damage. We were in trouble. I couldn't even move my arm to reach for my mark.

Peaches saw my epic landing and blinked out.

<No, boy! He's too strong.>

Oliver gestured and surrounded Peaches with a violet lattice as he reappeared a few feet away, mid-pounce.

"Good hellhound, stay." He swiped his hand, and Peaches crashed next to me, landing on his side.

<I can't go in between.>

<That's okay, boy. I'm working on a way out.>

<Will there be meat?>

<If we get out of this, you can have meat until you're tired of eating.>

He growled and rolled awkwardly to his feet, nudging closer to me.

Dex unleashed a green orb, followed by a barrage of black energy. Oliver gestured as he descended the stairs. A group of violet orbs intercepted Dex's attack, absorbed it, and raced at Dex.

"Where's your pigeon, Dex?" Oliver mocked as he directed the violet orbs. They split up, homing in on Dex as he ran for the alcove and threw up a defensive wall. The orbs floated in front of the green wall as Oliver continued down the steps. "Let me know if I should expect your goddess of a girlfriend. I have a special surprise for her."

He moved over to where Monty stood unsteadily. His pale face was covered in sweat. He used the wall for support as he focused on Oliver. He spat blood as Oliver stepped closer.

"Let my father go," Monty rasped, "before it's too late."

"Too late for what?" Oliver looked around. "You're planning on mounting an attack? You may have dispatched a few Envoys, and Arbiters, even some Ghosts. However, I have to say Wenk surprised me, he was quite skilled."

"Do it." Monty fell to one knee and coughed up more blood. He wiped away the blood from the ground.

"How does it feel to come home, Tristan? The familiar sights and smells… Well, it never smelled this scorched. Must bring back the memories."

"This was never my home. I was sent here to become a weapon, to become like you."

Oliver looked down at Monty, his expression one of disgust.

"Like me? You'll never be like me," Oliver hissed. "Oh, that's right, your home is with your beloved Nana. How is she these days? Still pulling the old 'I'm dead, but not really' trick?"

"She's no concern of yours."

"Again, you're mistaken, Tristan. Once I have control of the sects, once I've begun an age where mages rule this world, where our power is unquestioned, and we aren't hiding in the shadows, in temples, or remote mountains, and caves…. Once we're respected, then we'll deal with the mages like your Nana. And once she and those like her are gone, we'll take what's rightfully ours—everything."

"Humanity will never allow that. You'll start another war."

"Sometimes, in order to create, you must destroy. This is surely something you, of all mages, can understand."

"You're wrong." Monty coughed into his hand, wiping more blood off his hands and onto his pants. "I never destroy with the intention of creating. When I destroy, the intention, *my intention,* is to obliterate my target. When I create, the intention is to create."

"Well, we all can't be like the great Montague family."

Monty sat back against the wall. The image from the passage flashed in my mind.

"You...you always wanted to be a Montague," Monty answered, in between more blood-laden coughs. He swiped his hands along his pants again, and I noticed that he was down to one ring.

Oliver shook his head and tutted. "Tristan, you sound and look positively ill." He narrowed his eyes, examining Monty. "Are those traces of obsidian ice I see? Join me, and you'll be whole, truly whole. I can heal you and restore your ability to cast."

"Sod off!" Dex yelled. "He'll not be joining the likes of you, you sack of bollocks!"

Oliver glanced at Dex. "I wasn't speaking to you, you pathetic excuse for a mage." He gestured and slammed several of the orbs into Dex's shield, forcing Dex to focus on restoring it.

"Fuck you," I growled as I worked my way into a seated position, ignoring the searing agony of my bones knitting together as my body accelerated the healing. "In case it wasn't clear, he's not interested."

Oliver glanced my way with a smile and turned back to Monty. "I haven't heard from him yet. What do you say, Tristan? Join me and gain more power than you've ever imagined."

"Yes, I accept," Monty said quietly. "As long as you restore my casting and release my mother's essence."

"Once you provide me with the Archmage permutation, you'll be fully restored. As for your mother's essence, I never possessed it. I merely convinced your father I did."

"You never had it? How?"

Oliver shook his head. "I convinced Baudri to create a simulacra of her essence from some of her belongings your father treasured. It was an emotional resonance loop, not your mother's essence that he felt."

"It was an illusion?"

"A near perfect one." Oliver shook his head with a malicious smile. "Baudri was truly a master of his discipline. I had to eliminate him when he wanted to confess, the fool. That and he deceived me with a perfect copy of Ziller. I made him suffer for that. After I shift"—he looked around the courtyard—"I'll restore you and make sure their deaths are fast, no pain."

"Good," Monty said, wiping off more blood. "I don't want them to suffer."

"They won't. Come, join me."

I felt the shift almost immediately. I got to my feet and pulled at the lattice holding Peaches, but it wouldn't budge. I saw the last ring turn to dust around Monty's finger. I managed to get Ebonsoul under the lattice, cutting it, but it was slow going.

The blood around Monty and on his clothes burst with violet light. Monty got to his feet and, with a gesture, restored his clothing into an impeccable Zegna.

His energy signature was off the charts. It reminded me of the time we faced off against Julien. Monty had shifted to Archmage.

"You'll have to forgive me if I decline your offer."

"You traced the blood into the runes of permutation?" Oliver stepped back, surprised. "Clever, even for you, but you can't wield this power. It's too much for you."

"I'll be releasing my father now."

"No, I don't think so. I think you and your friends will be dying now. It's a pity, really. We could have ushered in a new era of magic. We could have ruled the world."

"The world doesn't need more rulers."

Oliver released an orb. It raced at Monty, who deflected it with a slap. It exploded on contact.

THIRTY-FIVE

WHEN THE SMOKE cleared, Oliver had disappeared. The lattice holding Peaches and the orbs attacking Dex vanished. We raced up the stairs. The figures in the circle lay in pools of blood. Connor Montague lay face down outside of the circle.

Monty ran over to where his father lay and slowly turned him over.

"You heard me," Connor said, his voice barely audible. "You created the permutation."

"I did," Monty replied quietly. "I don't know how you discovered this, but it's incredible, it's—"

"It's unstable, Tristan. I tried to explain it to Oliver, but he wouldn't listen. You have to release it, or it will kill you."

"I don't understand," Monty said, tracing some runes in the air. After a moment, he nodded. "It's imperfect."

Connor grabbed Monty by the arm and nodded. "There…there are no shortcuts. I was a fool for trying this, and a greater fool for allowing Oliver to deceive me with your mother."

"You heard? Of course, the bond."

Connor nodded. "No parent wants to bury their child, Tristan. Let the power go before it destroys you."

Monty stood up and flexed his fingers. Violet arcs raced across his arms and body.

"Connor, he's been exposed to obsidian ice." Dex looked at Monty. "If he releases the power, he'll die."

Connor looked at Monty and extended a hand. "I won't let him die. Let me help you release it, son."

Monty grabbed his father's hand and knelt beside him as they traced runes together. After a few moments, I felt another shift as Monty's energy signature nearly disappeared. He sagged forward and Dex caught him.

"Connor," Dex started.

"It's fine," Monty said, straightening out. "This is as it should be. Thank you, Father."

Connor held on to Monty's hand and stared into his face. Tears formed in the corners of his eyes and rolled down his cheeks.

"I'm sorry, son. I'm sorry for not being the father you deserved when you needed me."

"Father, you don't need to—"

Connor traced a rune on Monty's hand and whispered something under his breath. A golden band of light wrapped itself around both their hands, securing them together.

"Connor? What are you doing?" Dex said in agitation as he tried to separate them but couldn't. "Stop this. Stop this right now."

"Enough, Dex," Connor said gently, looking at his younger brother. "It's my choice. When I'm gone, it's up to you to restore this place."

"No, brother, don't." Dex shook his head. "Don't do this, we can help you. There has to be a way."

"It's too late for me, Dex. They've been draining my essence for a long time now."

"I'm sure there's a tome in the Repository that can reverse this," Monty said. "We can get Professor Ziller and he—"

Connor smiled and shook his head. "I'm not an Archmage any longer. Oliver and the remaining Elders saw to that, but what I have left, I give to you freely, son. I love you."

Connor traced runes in the air and the golden band exploded with light, temporarily blinding me. It lasted for several seconds before dying down and disappearing.

Connor was fading fast. His energy signature grew less noticeable with each second. He pulled Monty close with the last of his strength.

"Don't let him escape, Tristan. You stop Oliver or die in the attempt."

THIRTY-SIX

"WHAT DID HE do?" I looked around at the devastation. "Bloody hell."

"A transference. Connor transferred whatever was left of his essence to Tristan. How do you feel, lad?"

"I need you two to get back to the exit." Monty rested Connor gently on the ground, stood, and pulled on his sleeves. "I'll deal with Oliver."

"Not without us, you won't." Dex squared up against Monty, his face hard. "We'll stop him."

"No, I have to do this alone, don't you see? It was his dying wish."

Dex didn't budge. "His dying wish wasn't for you to join him, lad." He poked Monty in the chest. "You're not doing this alone. You may be cured of the ice, doesn't mean you can stand alone against Oliver."

"I can't."

"Of course you can't. That's why we're here."

"No, Uncle Dex, I can't lose anyone else. I have to do this alone. Oliver is too strong. I don't know if I'm walking away from this one."

"All the more reason for us to be by your side, lad. Now, find the bastard, and let's put an end to him."

Monty closed his eyes and slowed his breathing. "He's not in the Sanctuary." His eyes snapped open. "We need to get to the exit, now."

"I already told you, lad, we're not leaving your side," Dex started, and Monty grabbed him by the shoulder. "He went to the nexus. Oliver is in the nexus. He's trying to get off this plane."

We raced all the way to the bottom of the stairs, when it dawned on me that we would have to cross the Void Passage again. I stopped, quite abruptly, and Peaches almost threw my hip out of its socket.

Monty whirled on me.

"What is it? What part of urgency do you not understand? We have to stop him while he's in the nexus. It's our best chance."

"The fastest way through the Sanctuary is…?"

"The passage. We'll get you through it. Move, Simon."

"Not happening. Let me try something else. If it works, great. If not, I'll take the long way rather than go through that hell again."

"Now? Really?"

"Yes, now." I crouched down and placed my hands on the sides of Peaches' head.

<Do you remember how you caught Monty and put him on the ground?>

<Yes, he was like a big piece of sausage. You promised extra for that.>

<I did. Now I promise even more extra. Can you find the scary lady?>

He chuffed and shook his head. After a few seconds, he oriented himself and pointed his body in what I guessed was the direction of the Tushes.

<Yes, is she going to make me meat?>

<First, I need you to take us to her. Can you do that?>

<I can try.>

"Everyone grab the hellhound."

I held on to his collar as the runes in the stones began flashing. Monty looked concerned as he grabbed the collar too.

"Are you sure this is a good id—?"

The courtyard disappeared. A moment later, we were behind TK and LD.

"You know, of course, that you're cursed," TK was saying to LD. "May you live with an interesting wife."

"That is the only part of my life that is unquestionably not cursed."

"You lie so pretty," she said with her scary smile.

"Yes…I mean…no…I mean, it's a trap!" LD pointed behind her.

TK turned and unleashed a barrage of orbs at us. Monty waved an arm and deflected them to the side. TK raised an eyebrow, impressed.

"We need to get to the nexus, now."

LD stepped away from the wall and almost stumbled to the ground.

"He's nearly spent, but I think he can manage a portal." TK held him up. "Will you be able to get out on your own?"

I looked down at Peaches. "I'm pretty sure we can find a way off."

"In that case, stand together."

LD gestured, forming a gray circle under us. "Good to go."

"Remember your word, Tristan," TK said as they vanished.

THIRTY-SEVEN

ONCE WE ARRIVED at the nexus circle, an orb slammed into my side, sending me sprawling. Peaches blinked out as Oliver closed the distance, unleashing more orbs. Monty raised a shield while I tried to catch my breath from the bruised ribs.

"Ugh, I just got sucker orbed." I rubbed my side as my curse dealt with the injury. "Can we end him now?"

"We'd better. If he gets to our plane, he may be too strong, even for all of us. It has to be here and now."

Monty spun off to the side as I drew Grim Whisper and fired. Dex unleashed a wave of green energy as I pressed the bead on my mala and closed in on Oliver.

Oliver shifted sideways and avoided Dex's attack while simultaneously deflecting my bullets. Monty's orb crashed into his midsection and spun him around as Peaches blinked in, latched on to a leg, and proceeded to shake.

Dex unleashed a lattice and held him in place. Oliver tried futilely to break free, but the nexus had drained a large portion of his power.

"Once I'm free, I'll lay waste to your world."

Monty gestured and his hands gave off a golden glow as he approached.

"I'm going to make sure that doesn't happen."

Oliver glared as Monty knelt down next to him. "You wouldn't dare."

"Erasure is too good for him, lad. Put him out of his misery."

"No, Father would have offered him this mercy." Monty placed his hands on Oliver's temples. The golden light traveled from Monty hands to Oliver temples, and remained there, pulsing. Monty whispered something under his breath, and the golden glow transformed, turning darker. Peaches padded over to my side.

Oliver's screams filled the nexus for several minutes. Monty removed the gold band from Oliver's forehead, whispered once more, and disintegrated it.

"I will live to see the day you lie at my feet, begging for your life, Tristan Montague."

"You have no magic, I doubt you'll live that long."

<The bad man still smells bad. Can I bite him again?>

<What?>

I turned in time to see Oliver extend his arm and materialize a handcannon. He got off three shots: one grazed me in the arm, another punched through my leg, and the last one slammed into Dex.

"Shit, Dex!" He was still moving, but the pool of blood around his body was bad.

"Don't worry about me, finish him!" he yelled from the ground.

"Did you think you could erase me? You aren't the

only one who knows how to use reservoirs." Oliver held up a hand covered in rings. "You erased what I *allowed* you to erase."

"You bastard," Dex spat, clenching his midsection.

Oliver raised the handcannon again and took aim at Monty. "Goodbye, Tristan."

Monty shifted forward, gestured, and disappeared. He reappeared behind Oliver as he drew his swords, the Sorrows. Oliver tried to turn, but it was too late. Monty buried both of them through Oliver's chest. Their wails filled the nexus as Oliver fell to his knees, looking down in shock at the blades protruding from his chest.

The swords crackled with blue energy as Monty moved close and whispered something in Oliver's ear. Both swords erupted with power as Oliver's body disintegrated.

Monty sheathed his swords and ran over to Dex. He turned him over and placed a glowing hand over the wound.

"Don't you dare die on me, you old fool."

After a few moments, Dex coughed and cracked open an eye. "Next time, you check the bastard for reservoirs or any hidden weapons. What kind of battle mage are you? Are you just an expert at blowing up buildings? Didn't I teach you anything?"

"How did you do that?" I asked, once Monty made sure Dex would recover. "I've never seen you teleport like that."

"I'm just observant." He looked down at Peaches. "Your creature showed me how. I just needed to pay closer attention."

"Can we go home now? I could use about a decade

off."

I rested my head on the warm ground under me. My body was closing the wounds, and the warmth felt good for once.

"Before we start your vacation, you'll have to attend the reckoning as my shieldbearer."

"Can't you just apologize profusely for trying to Smith Bridge her, and call it a day?"

"Have you met TK?" He shook his head with an almost smile and then grew serious.

"Fine," I said, "but if she kills you, I'm not telling Roxanne."

"Simon, I wanted to say—"

"Save it. We're family. That's what family does for each other. Oh, and you both had better be ready to make sausage for days, until that hellhound explodes."

We headed to the circle. I looked up at the kaleidoscope sky one last time before it flashed, and we were gone…headed home.

THE END

CAST

CONNOR MONTAGUE-FATHER to Tristan and Elder of the Golden Circle.

Dex Montague-Uncle to Tristan, brother to Connor. One of the most powerful mages in the Golden Circle.

LD Tush Rogue Creative Mage, husband to TK Tush. Proprietor of Fordey Boutique. One of the Ten.

Ghosts-Mage Enforcers sent by the Golden Circle to pass judgement and apprehend or eliminate rogue mages. Tristan is currently being pursued by several of them.

Gideon the Ghost-Mages sent to escort rogue mages back to the Sanctuary. Tristan dispatched Gideon in a most painful manner now he's back and he's upset.

Gray Mages- Mages who serve Oliver Rank and can hide their energy signatures.

Grey Stryder-one of the last Night Wardens patrolling the city and keeping the streets safe. Current owner of *Kokutan no ken*.

Kali-(AKA Divine Mother) goddess of Time,

Creation, Destruction, and Power. Cursed Simon for unspecified reasons and has been known to hold a grudge. She is also one of the most powerful magic-users in existence.

Karma-The personification of causality, order, and balance. She reaps what you sow. Also known as the mistress of bad timing. Everyone knows the saying karma is a…some days that saying is true.

Living Library- A group of six ancient mages who act as repository of magical knowledge in very specific fields of study.

The Morrigan-Yes *that* Morrigan. Chooser of the Slain and currently in a relationship with Uncle Dex...don't ask.

Nana-Powerful sorceress and Tristan Montague's first instructor and nanny.

Noh Fan Yat- Martial arts instructor for the Montague & Strong Detective Agency. Teacher to both Simon and Tristan. Known for his bamboo staff of pain and correction.

Oliver Rank-Elder of the Golden Circle who attempted to seize power and take over the entire sect.

Peaches-(AKA Devildog, Hellhound, Arm Shredder and Destroyer of Limbs) Offspring of Cerberus and given to the Montague & Strong Detective Agency to help with their security. Closely resembles a Cane Corso-a very large Cane Corso.

Professor Ziller Mage responsible for the safeguarding of the Living Library and the Repository of knowledge at the Golden Circle. Don't try to have conversation with him…it will just melt your brain.

RJ-The team of Renè and Jonno. Two rogue mages

and pilots for the Ten. Don't mess with Renè's Strix.

Simon Strong-The intelligent (and dashingly handsome) half of the Montague & Strong Detective Agency. Cursed alive into immortality by the goddess Kali.

Steigh Cea Styne-one of the Jotnar entrusted with keeping the runic neutralizer safe. They thrive in ice and cold.

TK Tush Rogue Creative Mage, wife to LD Tush. Proprietor of Fordey Boutique. One of the Ten. She's not angry…really.

Tristan Montague- The civilized (and staggeringly brilliant) half of the Montague & Strong Detective Agency. Mage of the Golden Circle sect and currently on 'extended leave' from their ever-watchful supervision.

Wenk-Guardian of the Sanctuary. A Guardian is tasked with keeping the Sanctuary safe from any type of invasion—conventional or magical.

ORGANIZATIONS

FORDEY BOUTIQUE- ARTIFACT specialty store dealing in rare magical items that are usually dangerous and lethal, like the owners

New York Task Force-(AKA the NYTF) a quasi-military police force created to deal with any supernatural event occurring in New York City.

SuNaTran-(AKA Supernatural Transportations) Owned by Cecil Fairchild. Provides car and vehicle service to the supernatural community in addition to magic-users who can afford membership.

The Dark Council-Created to maintain the peace between humanity and the supernatural community shortly after the last Supernatural War. Its role is to be a check and balance against another war occurring. Not everyone in the Council favors peace.

Special Mentions for Homecoming

Laura C R. Because some things are just…Zillerific.

Jim Z. for Quantum Tunneling, nanogenerators and other timely mind melting topics we discuss at the right time and at the right moment. Spooky action at a distance!!

Cassandra for Peaches XL because it's perfect

Tammy and Larry for the inspiration for TK, LD and Fordey. L3 FTW Larry!!

Stacey S. for finding the staircase to heaven and having to die in this book. Good work!

Mel T. for the Kyorinrin. Paper dragons made of books and scrolls are awesome!

AUTHOR NOTES

THANK YOU FOR reading this story and jumping back into the world of Monty & Strong. This book touched a subject close to me, since I lost my father when I was seven. Thank you for allowing me to deal with that when I wrote this story. I didn't expect the feelings to resurface, but they did and I was able to get some closure through Monty and his dad.

With each book, I want to introduce you to different elements of the world Monty & Strong inhabit, slowly revealing who they are and why they make the choices they do. If you want to know how they met, that story is in NO GOD IS SAFE, which is a short explaining how Tristan and Simon worked their first case.

There are some references you will understand and some…you may not. This may be attributable to my age (I'm older than Monty or feel that way most mornings) or to my love of all things sci-fi and fantasy. As a reader, I've always enjoyed finding these "Easter Eggs" in the books I read. I hope you do too. If there is a reference you don't get, feel free to email me and I will explain it...maybe.

You will notice that Simon is still a smart-ass (deserving a large head smack) and many times he's clueless about what's going on. He's also acquired his first spell (an anemic magic missile!) even though he needs some practice with it. Bear with him—he's still new to the immortal, magical world he's been delicately shoved into. Fortunately he has Monty to nudge (or blast) him in the right direction.

Each book will reveal more about Monty & Strong's backgrounds and lives before they met. Rather than hit you with a whole history, I wanted you to learn about them slowly, the way we do with a person we just met— over time (and many large cups of DeathWish Coffee).

Thank you for taking the time to read this book. I wrote it for you and I hope you enjoyed spending a few more hours getting in (and out of) trouble with Tristan and Simon.

If you really enjoyed this story, I need you to do me a **HUGE** favor— **Please leave a review**.

It's really important and helps the book (and me). Plus, it means Peaches gets new titanium chew toys, besides my arms, legs, and assorted furniture to shred. And I get to keep him at normal size.

We want to keep Peaches happy, don't we?

CONTACT ME:

I REALLY DO appreciate your feedback. Let me
know what you thought by emailing me at:
www.orlando@orlandoasanchez.com
For more information on Monty & Strong…come
join the MoB Family on Facebook!
You can find us at:
Montague & Strong Case Files.
To get **FREE** stories visit my page at:
www.orlandoasanchez.com

STILL HERE? AMAZING! WELL, IF YOU'VE MADE IT THIS ...

INCLUDED IS THE first chapter of the next
Montague & Strong story-DRAGONS & DEMIGODS
here for you to read.
Enjoy!

DRAGONS AND DEMIGODS

A MONTAGUE AND Strong Book 6

All fathers are invisible in daytime; daytime is ruled by mothers and fathers come out at night. Darkness brings home fathers, with their real, unspeakable power. There is more to fathers than meets the eye. -Margaret Atwood

ONE

"MONTY, ARE YOU certain this is necessary?"

I looked up from the reports on my desk. Monty polished his swords, the Sorrows, and resheathed them. A soft cry escaped the blades as they disappeared into his back sheath.

"It's either this or we risk angering the entire family. This is the best solution."

"You know we need to address this Rott situation before he does something that gets him and us killed."

I remembered the last time I'd spoken to George Rott, Cassandra's father:

"You owe me, and you owe her."

"Listen, George, I don't know what you found, but why don't we meet to discuss this?"

"I found them," he whispered. "I found the dragons."

"We need to address this first." Monty pulled on one of his sleeves and reached for a cup of tea sitting on the desk. "They should be here shortly."

Between London and the Sanctuary, we hadn't been in the city for a week or so. Ramirez had left me messages about strange activity downtown near the Seaport. These events seemed to coincide with the increase in runic activity occurring near the Hellfire Club. I didn't like the timing, especially with George out hunting dragons.

I was about to call Ramirez, when a knock interrupted me.

"That them?" I holstered Grim Whisper and sheathed Ebonsoul. Peaches rolled over and nearly crushed my legs. I tried shoving him over, but he didn't budge.

<You could lie down anywhere else in the office, you know.>

<I know. But your feet are warm.>

The knock sounded again.

"Unless you're expecting your vampire, I would imagine so. I have one more item to secure before we leave. Can you let them in?"

I stood up and approached the door, when I saw the ice creep along the floor and enter the office.

"Monty? I think you need to get this one, unless we have a blowtorch handy?"

The temperature in the office dropped by twenty degrees and we entered a mini ice age as frost started to form on the door and creep around the frame.

"Are you ready?" he said, walking up to the door.

"For what, frostbite?"

He glared at me, reminding me that our guests weren't exactly friendly. He gestured and formed an orb of flame around his hand as he opened the door.

Three of the most beautiful women I'd seen in my entire life stood at our door. Three sets of sky-blue eyes blazed at us with thinly-veiled violence behind them.

Each of their faces was framed by white-blond hair. The fact that they wore combat armor under their long white leather coats did little to put me at ease.

Their energy signatures were strong enough to give me pause. Ice mages made me nervous after our brief but homicidal encounter with the not-so-stable Steigh Cea.

I hoped her sisters weren't as prone to spontaneous violence. The center woman, who was the tallest of the three, stepped into our office. The remaining two turned their backs on us and stayed outside the door.

"Well met, Hekla," Monty said with a nod. "Will all of you be joining us?"

Hekla nodded and took in our office, remaining silent for a few seconds. Her eyes lingered over Peaches and she sniffed with a hint of disgust. Maybe it was an ice mage thing, but she had the condescending look down to an art form. I almost wanted to run to my room and straighten it out.

"I'm here to secure the runic neutralizer, mage," she said, her husky voice filling the office. "If I deem your location of choice to be inadequate, I will relocate it to our home, as per out agreement. My sisters will remain here until I return."

"Understood." Monty gestured and formed a large circle on the floor. "We will be traveling to Fordey Boutique. I have chosen them to keep the neutralizer safe and I have some matters to attend to there."

"Proceed." She waved her hand as if we were boring her just by existing. "Do you need assistance with your circle?"

"Thank you for the offer, but I believe I can

manage."

She looked down when Peaches stepped into the circle with us. "This infernal *thing* will be traveling with us?"

"He has a habit of following me around," I said, barely containing my anger. I rubbed Peaches' head. "It's better if *Peaches* joins us."

She stepped to the other side of the circle and nodded to Monty. "Carry on, mage."

Monty gestured as white runes floated around us. With a last sweep of his arm, the office disappeared.

ACKNOWLEDGMENTS

I'm finally beginning to understand that each book, each creative expression usually has a large group of people behind it. This story is no different. So let me take a moment to acknowledge my (very large) group:

To Dolly: my wife and biggest fan. You make all of this possible and keep me grounded, especially when I get into my writing to the exclusion of everything else. Thank you, I love you.

To my Tribe: You are the reason I have stories to tell. You cannot possibly fathom how much and how deep I love you all.

To Lee: Because you were the first audience I ever had. I love you sis.

To the Logsdon family: JL your support always demands I bring my A-game and produce the best story I can. I always hear: "Don't rush!" in your voice.

L.L. (the Uber Jeditor) your notes and comments turned this story from good to great. I accept the challenge!

Your patience knows no bounds. Thank you both.

Arigatogozaimasu

The Montague & Strong Case Files Group AKA- The MoB(The Mages of BadAssery)

When I wrote T&B there were fifty-five members in The MoB. As of this writing there are 543 members in the MoB. I am honored to be able to call you my MoB Family. Thank you for being part of this group and M&S. You each make it possible.

THANK YOU.

<u>WTA-The Incorrigibles</u>

JL,BenZ, EricQK, S.S., and the Mac

They sound like a bunch of badass misfits because they are. My exposure to the slightly deranged and extremely deviant brain trust that you are made this book possible. I humbly thank you and…it's all your fault.

<u>The English Advisory</u>

Aaron, Penny, Carrie

For all things English..thank you.

<u>**DEATH WISH COFFEE**</u>

Kane & Sierra- Thank you!

Is there any other coffee on the face of the earth that can compare? I think not.

<u>To Deranged Doctor Design</u>

Kim. Darja, Milo

You define professionalism and creativity. Thank you for the great service and amazing covers.

YOU GUYS RULE!

<u>To you the reader</u>:

Thank you for jumping down the rabbit hole with me. I truly hope you enjoy this story. You are the reason I wrote it.

ART SHREDDERS

No book is the work of just one person. I am fortunate enough to have an excellent team of readers and shredders who give of their time and keen eyes to provide notes, insight, and corrections. They help make this book go from good to great. Each and every one of you helped make this book fantastic.

THANK YOU

Amanda H. Amanda S. Amy R. Audra V. M. Barbara H. Beau W. Bennah P. Beverly C. Brandi Moore L. Brandy D. Brenda Nix L. Caroline L. Carrie Anne O. Cassandra H. Charlotte C. Chris B. Chris C II. Claudia L-S. Corrine L. Daniel P. Darren M. Davina N. Dawn McQ. M. Denise K. Donald T.

Heather H. Helen V. Jen C. Jennifer W.
Jim S. Joscelyn S. Kandice S. Karen H
Karen H. Karla H. Kevin M. Kimbra S.
Klaire T. Larry Diaz T. Laura Cadger R.
Laura Maria R. Lesley S. Linda W. Liz
C. Marie McC. Mary Anne P. MaryAnn
S. Marydot Hoffecker P. Melody DeL.
Michelle S. Mike H. Natalie F. Noah S.
Oddegeir O L. RC B. Rene C.
Robert"The Question" W. Samantha L.
Sara Mason B. Scott O. Shawnie N.
Stacey S. Stephanie C. Steve Woofie W.
Sue W. Tami C. Tammy Ashwin K.
Tammy T. Terri A. Thomas R. Timothy
L. Tommy O. Tracy B. Tracy M. Violet
F. Wendy S.

Thank You!

If you enjoyed this book, would you please help me by leaving a review at the site where you purchased it from? It only needs to be a sentence or two and it would really help me out a lot!

All of My Books

The Warriors of the Way
The Karashihan* • Spiritual Warriors • The Ascendants • The Fallen Warrior • The Warrior Ascendant • The Master Warrior

John Kane
The Deepest Cut* • Blur

Sepia Blue
The Last Dance* • Rise of the Night

Chronicles of the Modern Mystics
The Dark Flame • A Dream of Ashes

Montague & Strong Detective Agency
Tombyards & Butterflies• Full Moon Howl•Blood Is Thicker• Silver Clouds Dirty Sky • Homecoming• NoGod is Safe•The Date•The War Mage

Night Warden
Wander

Books denoted with an asterisk are FREE via my website.
www.OrlandoASanchez.com

ABOUT THE AUTHOR

Orlando Sanchez has been writing ever since his teens when he was immersed in creating scenarios for playing Dungeon and Dragons with his friends every weekend. An avid reader, his influences are too numerous to list here. Some of the most prominent are: J.R.R. Tolkien, Jim Butcher, Kat Richardson, Terry Pratchett, Christopher Moore,Terry Brooks, Piers Anthony, Lee Child, George Lucas, Andrew Vachss, and Barry Eisler to name a few in no particular order.

The worlds of his books are urban settings with a twist of the paranormal lurking just behind the scenes and generous doses of magic, martial arts, and mayhem.

Aside from writing, he holds a 2nd and 3rd Dan in two distinct styles of Karate. If not training, he is studying some aspect of the martial arts or martial arts philosophy.

He currently resides in Queens, NY with his wife and children and can often be found in the local Starbucks where most of his writing is done.

Please visit his site at OrlandoASanchez.com for more information about his books and upcoming releases.

Made in the USA
Las Vegas, NV
28 January 2022

42545553R10173